The Old West R...

VAN HOLT

THE REVENGE OF TOM GRABEN

Ride the Old West

CHAPTER 1

Frank Graben stopped his blue roan gelding among some rocks on a
bleak barren ridge top and studied the country around him with his
gray eyes narrowed to glittering slits. His face was bony and darkly
weathered. His dark hair had a copper tinge. He wore a flat-crowned
black hat, a double-breasted black shirt and black trousers. There
was a brown corduroy coat tied behind his saddle. He packed his
Smith & Wesson .44 Russian pistols in tied-down holsters.

There were enemies looking for him, and he had no friends anywhere. He kept to himself and there was something about him that
kept most people at a distance. Those who ventured closer were usually looking for trouble, and they usually found it.

Two days before at dusk he had stopped at a place called Turley's,
a combination store and saloon. Several bearded, rough-garbed men
stood at the bar drinking when Graben came in through the swing
doors and stopped near the front end of the bar to drink a beer in
silence. He did not appear to notice the men but he was aware that
they were sizing him up in the back-bar mirror and grinning at one
another in a way that spelled trouble. So he finished his beer and
went through a doorway into the store to get a sack of grub and a few
other things he needed.

When he came back out the five men had left the saloon and were
standing outside, near his horse. They were still grinning but there
was nothing friendly in their grins. Graben went around them and

tied the grub sack to the horn of his saddle in frowning silence, then stepped into the saddle.

"Where'd you get that horse, mister?" one of them said then. It was the youngest of the five, a beardless boy still in his teens.

Graben merely stared at him through cold narrowed eyes and did not bother to answer. A couple of the others took a closer look at him and shifted their feet uncomfortably, perhaps sensing that he was nobody to fool around with. But the kid saw only himself and he liked what he saw.

His voice rose a little. "I'm talkin' to you, mister! I said where did you get that horse?"

Graben still remained silent, watching the boy, watching them all, and it was plain by then that his unexpected silence was getting on their nerves.

The boy's voice was a little shrill as he said, "That there's my horse, mister! He was stole from me a while back!"

Graben merely lifted the reins and started to turn the roan, and as he did so the boy yelled something and went for his gun. A moment later he lay dead in the dirt and Graben's smoking revolver was trained on the others.

"Anybody else think I'm a horse thief?" he asked.

They eyed the gun uneasily and shook their heads.

Then, as Graben backed the horse across the road, still keeping them covered, one of them said, "I shore wouldn't want to be in yore place, mister. That was Tobe Unger's kid brother you killed."

Graben did not know who Tobe Unger was and he did not bother to ask, but he judged that he was somebody to reckon with, or thought he was, and would no doubt be coming after Graben as soon as he heard. And the men who had seen the shooting would be with him. If Graben did not miss his guess, they were already on his trail, and might even circle ahead to set up an ambush.

That was why he studied the old shack with care before riding down the rocky slope toward it. The shack was as weathered and gray as the rocks around it, and looked abandoned. No smoke rose from the rock chimney, there were no horses in the sagging pole corral, and the glassless windows were just empty shadowy holes, like eyes watching him.

For some reason, the place made him uneasy. But he decided he was just jumpy as a result of killing a boy who apparently had a mean, tough brother, and several friends who looked like pirates in western garb.

When he did approach the shack it was by circling down through the rocks and coming up on the shack's blind side, where there were no windows. He might have saved himself the trouble, for when he got inside he found wide cracks between the unchinked logs through which anyone in the one-room shack could have seen him. But there was no one inside the shack and it did not appear that there had been anyone here for some time. The rough plank floor was covered with dust and debris and the stone fireplace was about the same, a good indication that it had not been used recently.

Graben went back outside to the well and drew up the wooden bucket on its frayed, half-rotten rope. There was no water in the bucket. It was half full of sand.

A piercing cackle caused him to drop the bucket and spin around, whipping out a gun. A woman had just emerged from the rocks leading a saddled horse. The sun was directly in Graben's slitted eyes and he could not tell whether the woman's sun-cured face was young or old, whether her hair was gray or sun-bleached blond. But he could tell that she was laughing at him.

"Ain't no water in that well, mister," she said, limping toward him. "Ain't been for years."

Graben's narrow eyes studied the rocks behind her, and seeing this she cackled again and said, "Don't worry, I'm by myself, more's the pity. Nobody wants nothin' to do with Crazy Cora."

She sat down on the ground, tugged off her right boot and rubbed her foot with a callused hand. Graben saw now that she was somewhere in her middle years, but he could not narrow it down much closer than that.

"My horse picked up a limp a piece back," she said with a rueful grin. "Now it looks like I've picked up one, too."

Graben remained silent and she glanced up to study his lean hard face and cold slitted eyes. "I got a place farther back in the hills," she said, hooking a thumb over her shoulder. "Sometimes I come over this way lookin' for strays. Stray men, that is."

She cackled again, but there was no trace of a smile in Graben's eyes. He had not wanted to run into anyone, much less a crazy, man-hunting old woman.

Turning away without a word, he went toward his horse.

"Hey, hold on a minute, mister," she said. "I didn't mean to alarm you. I ain't in the habit of ropin' and brandin' any of the men I see. I just try to find out if they've seen my daughter. She run off with that no-account Tobe Unger three months back and I ain't seen her since."

Graben stopped and turned to look at the woman and he was surprised to see that her faded eyes were damp. Perhaps she was not as crazy as she seemed. "Unger hang ground here much?" he asked.

"Not no more," she said bitterly. "He used to hang around my place all the time till he got my Gibby to run off with him."

"Gibby?"

Crazy Cora tugged off her other boot and massaged that foot also. "I just knowed it was gonna be a boy, and I was gonna name him Gib after his no-account pa what done run off on me. Only it weren't no him, and I named *her* Gibby. Purtiest baby I ever did see and she just got purtier and purtier as she growed up. All I could do to keep men away from her. Wouldn't never allow no men around there on account of her. But that no-account Tobe Unger tricked me, when I should of knowed what he was after. He let on like he was sweet on me, when all he wanted was to use my place for a hideout for him and his gang and to sweet-talk my Gibby behind my back. He ever comes back around, I aim to empty my shotgun at him."

She gestured toward her horse and Graben saw the gun in the saddle scabbard.

"Don't reckon you've seen anything of them?" she asked. "Gibby's a towhead with light green eyes and the cutest baby face you ever saw. Sometimes it don't seem rightly possible that she could be my girl. She's just seventeen and Tobe Unger's more'n twice that, and a big ugly mean-lookin' rascal. What a girl like her ever saw in him I don't know. Course, in my case there weren't too many men to pick and choose from. But Gibby could of had any man she wanted, and someday the right one would of turned up, and I wouldn't of run him off like I did the others. I kept tellin' her that. Just be patient a while longer, I told her. Don't run off with the first sweet-talkin' rascal that comes along like I did. You'll live to regret it if you do.

"But I never thought to warn her about Tobe Unger, and I sure never thought about him pullin' the wool over my eyes the way he did neither. I knowed he was mean as a snake, but I thought it was all out in the open. He just never seemed to me like the cunnin' type, and when he made such a fuss over my Gibby I just thought it was all in good-natured fun and that he was tryin' to cheer her up 'cause the pore girl always seemed so lonesome without nobody her own age around to talk to. But I guess I should of knowed what he was after all along."

Graben stood by his horse with the reins in his hand, a look of growing impatience in his eyes. He felt sorry for the old woman in a general way, but there was nothing he could do for her, and he did not have time to listen to her troubles. He had his own to worry about, and every moment he remained here increased his danger.

"I haven't seen anyone who looked like your daughter," he said. Then he asked, "Maybe you could tell me where's the nearest water?"

"The nearest water," she said, "is at my place."

Crazy Cora's place turned out to be only a few miles away, and she decided that her horse's feet were in better shape to walk that distance than her own were. En route she explained to Graben that she and "Gib" had squatted on the only sweet waterhole around right after they were married and had hauled logs from mountains thirty miles away to build their one-room cabin, later adding a lean-to kitchen. But in spite of this addition the house turned out to be only a fraction larger than the shack they had just left, and Graben wondered, but did not ask, how they had all managed to crowd into the place when the Unger gang was around. Where had two women and half a dozen men slept? Perhaps the men had slept outside.

The house and waterhole were in a little pocket surrounded by brushy, rocky hills. The area was littered with rocks and boulders that had tumbled down, and Crazy Cora sat down on a nearby rock and watched Graben as he squatted down to fill his canteen while his horse drank beside him. When the woman suddenly let out one of her startling, unexpected cackles, he raised his head and looked at her through cold half-lidded eyes, wondering again if she was as crazy as her nickname implied.

"I was just thinkin' about the look on your face over there when you drawed up that bucket of sand," she said. "What's your name anyway? I know a body ain't supposed to ask, but you don't have to give me your real name. I'd just like to know something to call you when I tell folks about runnin' into you over there and that look on your face."

"Why don't you just make one up for me?" Graben suggested.

She studied him for a moment and then said, "I think I'll call you Graben."

Graben gave her a startled glance. "Why Graben?"

"You remind me of a fellow named Graben who come through

here a few months back," she said, again studying his face. "In some
ways he looked a lot like you. Tall like you, same color of hair. I think
his eyes was more blue than yours. I guess you'd call yours gray,
wouldn't you?"

"I would. Some people call them blue."

He pulled his horse back from the water and hung his canteen on
the horn. His back to Crazy Cora, he asked, "You happen to catch his
first name?"

"Seems like it was Tom," she said. "Yeah, that's what it was, Tom
Graben."

Graben had started to tighten his cinch. Now he loosened it again
and sat down on a rock not far from Crazy Cora. "That fellow happen
to say where he was headed?"

"He never said," Crazy Cora told him. "But it don't matter none,
'cause he never got there, wherever it was."

Graben glanced at her leathery face and bright pale eyes. "What
makes you think that?" he asked in the same idle tone as before.

Crazy Cora's own voice dropped to a conspiratorial whisper. "I
never meant to tell nobody, but now I don't care who knows about it.
They killed him, Tobe and the others did. They thought he was some
kind of law snoopin' around, so they killed him."

Graben was prepared for that and there was no change on his
bleak weathered face. He showed nothing more than idle curiosity.
"Fair fight?"

There was utter scorn in Crazy Cora's pale eyes. "Nah! He looked
plumb dangerous, that one did. Them pale cold blue eyes could look
right through you and send a chill down your spine. So they didn't
take no chances. Shot him down from behind as he started to get on
his horse, that fine buckskin Dub Astin still rides. They played poker
for his horse and saddle and his guns. Dub got the horse and saddle
and Zeke Fossett got the guns."

Frank Graben sat on the rock thinking about what the woman
had told him. So Tom was dead, he thought. Tom had been two years
older than Frank, and more of a man than he would ever be, but a
loner like himself. As boys growing up back in Missouri they had
been close, but they had had their differences and had gone their
separate ways after their parents died and the farm was sold. Frank
had not seen or heard from Tom since, and now he would never see
him again.

"Funny thing though," he heard Crazy Cora say. "They took his body back up in the hills yonder and just left him there. A few days later they got to thinkin' maybe they should of hid the body better and went back up there to do the job right. But they never did find him. It was night when they took him up there and left him and it had come a big rain so there wasn't no tracks they could foller back to where they was before. We never could figger out whether they just couldn't find where they left him, or whether somebody had rode by the next day and decided to take him into Rock Crossin' or someplace and bury him decent. We kept expectin' to hear something about it, but we never did, and you can believe we never asked nobody about it."

"No, I guess not," Frank Graben grunted, his eyes unbelievably cold. As cold, Crazy Cora was thinking, as Tom Graben's eyes.

Frank got to his feet and glanced at the unpainted log house. "Anybody else here that night?"

"Mac Radner was here, playin' cards with Tobe and them." She hooked a thumb over her shoulder. "Mac and his two brothers has got them a little place back over here a piece. They call theirselves horse ranchers, but they stole most of them horses. And sometimes they ride with Tobe and the boys if they're wanted or needed."

"Well, I better push on," Graben said, going toward his horse.

Crazy Cora went to her own horse and casually pulled the double barrel shotgun from the scabbard. Graben watched her uneasily, but she made no threatening gesture with the gun and he assumed that she meant to take it inside after he left. "No call to rush off," she said. "I aim to rustle up some chuck here before long, and I might even let you spend the night, if you was lonesome for a little company."

Her sudden cackle made him wince. "I'm not that lonesome," he said, scowling, and stepped into the saddle. "Thanks for the water."

Crazy Cora merely nodded, silent for a change, and watched him turn his horse to ride off. She noticed that he was heading back the way they had come a little earlier, but she did not think anything about it.

She watched him until he was almost out of range, and then she brought up the sawed-off shotgun and fired both barrels at his back, aiming high enough not to hit the horse. Crazy Cora liked horses, but she had no use for men who had no use for her.

She saw the stranger slump forward in the saddle, but somehow he hung on and got the horse into a gallop along the narrow winding valley through which the trail ran.

"He won't git far!" Crazy Cora shrieked, dancing with glee. "Crazy

Cora can do it just as good as Tobe and them! I'd go after him, Bess, if you wasn't all gimpy like me!"

Frank Graben did not know how he managed to stay in the saddle, or how far he rode. He was barely conscious most of the time. The horse slowed to a trot and then to a walk, and finally stopped, and he became dimly aware that four rough-looking men sat their horses before him, blocking the trail.

"Well, look who we got here," one of them said in a taunting, vaguely familiar voice. "Tobe is gonna be real pleased when he finds out we done got the man what killed Chip."

"Looks like Crazy Cora already put some buckshot in him," another chuckled.

"Hell, let's finish the bastard and get it over with," said a third.

He could not see their faces clearly, because the light was fading and he could not get his eyes into proper focus for some reason. But now he knew who they were, and he knew they meant to kill him. His hand groped for his gun and found the butt, but the gun seemed to weigh a ton and he did not have the strength to lift it.

Then all four of them were shooting into him and he was falling from the saddle.

A tall man stood up in the rocks on the rough slope above Graben and began firing, the dark long-barreled pistol bucking in his fist. Two of the riders tumbled out of their saddles and the other two turned their horses and spurred away. The tall man in the rocks fired one shot after them and then his gun clicked on an empty chamber.

A minute later Frank Graben found the tall man bending over him. He peered up into the lean weathered face and cold pale blue eyes of Tom Graben. And that gaunt stubbled face was the last thing Frank Graben saw before he died.

CHAPTER 2

Dub Astin and Zeke Fossett were almost a third of the way back to Turley's when they met three riders approaching along the dark trail. Dub and Zeke skidded their lathered horses to a halt and jerked out their guns before they recognized Tobe Unger's bellow of rage. The two men with Unger were Barney Kester and Clyde Picker.

"Fools!" Unger roared. "Why are you killin' them horses?"

"Sorry, Tobe," Zeke Fossett apologized, holstering the gun that had once belonged to Tom Graben. "Didn't recognize you in the dark."

"What's got you boys spooked?" the big man growled. "And where's Tim and Shorty?"

"Shot all to hell!" Dub Astin cried. "Tom Graben killed them!"

"Get hold of yourself," Tobe Unger barked. "Tom Graben's dead."

"Dead or not, it was him! But we got the man who killed Chip. He was comin' back this way, but he prob'ly didn't even know where he was goin'. It looked like Crazy Cora had already filled him full of buckshot. Then Tom Graben stepped out of them rocks and started shootin'—"

"Hold on here," Unger interrupted. "Calm down and tell me what happened.

"I just did!" Dub Astin cried. "We soon lost that feller's trail, but it was headin' toward Crazy Cora's place and we figgered he'd stop there for water, so we headed that way as fast as we could go and when we were almost there we met him comin' back. He was almost layin' down on the horn and barely conscious, but he tried to draw on us and we filled him full of lead. That was when Tom Graben started shootin' at us from the rocks. Tim and Shorty was closer to him and they was killed in the first blast. Me and Zeke weren't fightin' no ghost, so we got the hell out of there."

"It wasn't no ghost," Tobe Unger said heavily. "I always wondered why we couldn't find his body when we went to look for it. I don't know how he could still be alive after we put all that lead in him, but somehow he is, and now we've got to do the job over."

Working by moonlight, Tom Graben buried his dead brother that night. He buried Frank in a place where no man was likely to find him, and covered him with rocks so no wolf or vulture could get at him.

He kept Frank's wallet, his belt and guns, and the corduroy coat. He did not think Frank would have minded. And the blue roan gelding. Tom Graben needed the horse. The animal he had been riding lately was a bit of an embarrassment, and would probably cave in if pushed too hard.

He also kept the guns and cartridge belts that had belonged to the dead Tim and Shorty and cached them in a convenient place, should he ever need them. He figured those two owed him. But he had unsaddled their horses and turned them loose, for he figured the horses were stolen, and stolen horses were hard to explain from the end of a rope, with the noose cutting off your wind. Tom Graben had seen it tried, but not successfully.

The grave was in a depression at the base of a cliff, and he arranged the rocks over it to look as if they had tumbled down from the rim above. He would be able to find the spot again himself, and he doubted if there was anyone else who cared. Frank had been a loner like himself and had not made friends easily.

When the grave was finished and disguised to his satisfaction, Tom Graben sat down on a nearby rock, feeling lost and empty inside. He kept thinking about all the things he and Frank had said to each other when they were boys growing up on that poor rocky farm back in Missouri, things that never should have been said, and all the things that should have been said but had not been. Finally they had quit talking to each other except for the few words that could not very well be avoided. Mostly they had worked the unyielding fields in silence, not speaking for fear they might say something they would regret. Their father had lost an arm at Gettysburg and had used it as an excuse not to do any work and their mother had been sick a lot, so the two boys had had to do most of the work on the farm, and in the winter, after the crops were in, they had hired out when they could and had cut and hauled firewood for people when they could not find any other work.

Life had not been easy and there was a strange ache inside Tom Graben when he thought about those long hard days when he and Frank had worked side by side almost without speaking. They had felt closer to each other than to anyone else, and yet that awful silence had been there between them, like an ever widening gulf that neither could bridge.

After their parents died there had seemed no point in keeping the exhausted farm. They had sold it and gone their separate ways, parting with a few brief casual words, still unable or afraid to say what was inside them. Since then they had not seen each other.

Not until a little after sundown today, when Frank, already badly wounded, had ridden past the spot where Tom was waiting for the four men approaching from the opposite direction. Tom had held his fire for fear of endangering Frank until it was too late to do him any good. It had not occurred to Tom that the four might try to kill another Graben, who was already so badly wounded. He had even been fool enough to think they might show a spark of humanity and even try to help Frank. Instead they had finished killing him. Frank had lived only a few seconds after Tom reached him. There had been no time then to say any of the things that should have been said so long ago, and now Tom would never know if it would have been possible anyway for him or Frank to say any of those things.

That they happened to be in the same place at that particular moment, after not seeing each other for over ten years, was one of those strange, unexplainable things that sometimes happened in real life, but which no one would believe if put in a book. It almost made a man wonder if there might be such a thing as fate after all.

To Tom Graben it seemed a bitter irony, like a mocking reminder that you could not put something off forever and still count on having time to get it done at the last moment.

He got to his feet with a weary sigh and went over to Frank's saddled horse standing with the reins down. Tom had already turned his crowbait loose and hoped he would never set eyes on the sorry beast again.

Frank's cartridge belt and holstered revolvers hung from the saddle horn. Tom took the guns down and buckled them on and tied the holsters down. His own gun was thrust in his waistband where he had been carrying it, expecting soon to recover the cartridge belt and guns that had been taken from him after they had shot him.

The night had turned chilly and he untied the corduroy coat from behind the saddle and put it on. He had been getting by with a vest. The coat fitted him perfectly. Frank had grown about an inch after leaving home at seventeen, and Tom kept thinking what a fine looking man his brother had become, and how it was so bad for a man like that to be cut down in his prime. Frank had been only twenty-eight. But he would never get any older.

By rights I should be the one in that grave, Tom Graben thought, as he mounted the blue roan and headed for the cave where he had been holed up now for over a week, waiting for the Unger gang to return.

In the cave later he found a change of clothes rolled up in Frank's blankets. There was a double-breasted blue shirt like the one Frank had been wearing except for the color, and a pair of trousers that were so dark a gray that he thought at first they were black. He tried the clothes on and found that they fitted as well as the corduroy coat.

In one of the saddlebags there was a small coffeepot, a frying pan, a tin cup and a tin plate, and in the grub sack there were several things Tom was running short of, coffee, flour, bacon, beans, jerky and hardtack.

He boiled a pot of coffee and sitting by the fire later he counted the money in Frank's wallet. A little over five hundred dollars. Frank had been doing all right financially. You did not run into very many people with that much money in their pocket. It was more money than Tom Graben had seen in quite a while. He hoped Frank had come by it honestly, but he might never know for sure. The boy he had known wouldn't have robbed anyone but a robber or cheated anyone who wasn't trying to cheat him, but he didn't know how much Frank had changed since then.

In the other saddlebag Tom found several pairs of socks, a new black bandanna, some underwear, a box of cartridges, and a pocket knife carefully wrapped in oilskin. He studied the knife with interest, as if he had never seen it before, although he had given the knife to Frank one Christmas when they were boys, before the silence came between them. Frank had kept the knife all these years, in a like-new condition. It seemed out of character somehow, for Frank had never seemed much the sentimental type. But it was something for Tom Graben to wonder about as he sat by the fire thinking about his dead brother.

Since killing Tim and Shorty he had not thought much about what he would do about the other two, Dub Astin and Zeke Fossett. He had already planned to kill them and now he had another reason for doing so. He did not yet know what he would do about Crazy Cora, who must have put the buckshot in Frank's back.

Unknown to him, the problem of Crazy Cora was solved for him the next morning when what was left of the Unger gang rode up to her shack. Crazy Cora came out with her shotgun and screeched at them before they had a chance to dismount. "Tobe Unger, what have you done with my daughter?"

"I left her at Turley's," the big man growled. "She's been cryin' and whinin' to come home and see her mama, and I was afraid I'd have a time gettin' her away from here if I let her come back. If I'd knowed she was gonna be such a baby I never would of bothered with her, at least not till she growed up. But once I slap my brand on something it stays mine, and she might as well get used to the idea. You might as well get used to it too, Crazy Cora," he added, scowling at the old woman's twisted face.

Crazy Cora shrieked at him, "You better bring my daughter back home to her mama where she belongs, you no-account, girl-rustlin' son of a two-bit whore!"

Without waiting for a reply, Crazy Cora started bringing up the scattergun.

With a hoarse cry of rage, Tobe Unger clawed out a big pistol and blasted her back against the log wall of the shack. She slid down the wall to the ground and the big man swung down from his saddle and strode toward her. "Crazy old fool!" he shouted when he concluded that she was dead, and he gave her a good kick in sheer frustration. "I never meant to kill the old bitch, but she didn't give me no choice."

"You can't blame yoreself, Tobe," Dub Astin told him. "She had it comin'."

Tobe Unger stared at all four of them with hard narrow eyes. "Listen, you bastards, and listen good. When Gibby finds out about this, it wasn't me who killed Crazy Cora. It was Tom Graben. You all got that?"

They all nodded and Astin, the talker of the group, said, "Sure,

Tobe. Whatever you say."

"Just remember that," Unger said, glancing at the dead woman. "It wasn't my fault, but Gibby wouldn't believe it. She's as bullheaded in some ways as her ma was."

He glanced at the sun rising over the barren gray mountains to the east and thought for a moment. "Dub, you ride over and tell the Radner boys they better keep a eye peeled. Mac was over here that night and Graben will prob'ly be gunnin' for him too. If Graben's as hard to find as I figger he'll be, we may need them to help us comb that rough country. And tell them to keep some fresh horses handy. We'll likely need them before long. We could use some right now as a matter of fact, especially you and Zeke could."

"Why don't I get them boys to come on back over here with me and bring some horses with us?" Astin said. "I know they'll want in on this."

Unger's thick dark brows knitted in a frown. He did not like suggestions and he did not like anyone trying to help him do his thinking. He was the boss and the brains of this outfit. But after a moment he shrugged. "Might as well, I guess," he said. "But hurry on back over here. I want to start lookin' just as soon as we can round up some chuck and pile some rocks over Crazy Cora."

Dub Astin nodded and took the narrow trail that wound through the barren rocky hills to the Radner place three miles to the south. Nothing grew among the rocks but a few stunted cedars, forever harried by the lonesome wind and twisted into strange, tortured shapes.

Astin was no more than half a mile from Crazy Cora's shack when Tom Graben suddenly appeared on the rocky slope a little above him and to his right. Astin had no idea where the tall lean man had come from. It was as if he had materialized from thin air, the way it was said that a ghost could materialize. A ghost whose spirit could not rest because of something that had happened while he was alive, some unfinished business that he had to return to finish before he could find peace.

There was a gun in Graben's hand and a look in his cold pale blue eyes that froze Dub Astin's heart with fear. Remembering what had happened to Tim and Shorty, Astin felt a wild, almost overwhelming impulse to turn the buckskin and ride for his life. But he knew if he did that he would die, and he knew if he reached for a gun he would die. So he did neither. He reined the horse in and kept his hand well away from his gun, hoping that if he showed no fight Graben would not kill him, at least not now. Astin knew he would die someday, but he wanted to put it off as long as he could.

Astin noticed that Graben was wearing the shell belt and holstered Russian pistols that the stranger had been wearing at Turley's and on the trail late yesterday when Astin and the others had killed him, or finished killing him. But the cocked pistol in Graben's hand was a Colt and appeared to be one of those open-top .44s that had come out a year or two before the Peacemaker. The dark barrel seemed incredibly long, although Astin had never seen a gun of that type with a barrel longer than eight inches. But that was long enough.

Then Astin remembered that the guns they had taken off the apparently dead Graben had been open-top Colts. Zeke Fossett still had one of them. He had traded the other one to the storekeeper in Rock Crossing for a suit of clothes. And Dub Astin had a hunch that the gun Tom Graben now held in his hand was the one Fossett had traded off. It had been thrust in Graben's waistband that evening when he had stopped at Crazy Cora's for water and a meal, and that was one reason why Zeke had traded it off; he had no holster for it.

And as Tom Graben continued to stare at him in silence through those cold pale blue eyes, another thought occurred to Astin. Graben bore a striking resemblance to the stranger they had killed. He wondered why he had not noticed it before. The eyes were different and the brown hair had more of a yellowish-copper tinge, but the lean weathered face, the straight nose and thin hard mouth reminded Astin of the man they had murdered, and a new fear crept through him. If the dead man had been Tom Graben's brother, then Astin's chances of getting away from here alive were very slim indeed.

As if reading his thoughts, Graben said, "If you're wondering why you're not already dead, I'll tell you. I want you to take a message back to the others, and I also want to look forward to killing you later. But you can walk back. Get down off my horse and saddle. On this side where I can see you. Buck won't mind for a change."

Astin climbed awkwardly down on the right side of the horse and stood waiting for further instructions, uneasily watching the tall man up in the rocks. With most men he would have tried to talk his way out of the fix he was in, but he had a feeling amounting almost to certainty that the less he said to Tom Graben the better. Graben would not listen to anything he might have to say in the way of excuses.

Graben's eyes seemed to get even colder as he said, "What happened to my money and my guns?"

Dub Astin shifted his feet uneasily. "Tobe Unger took the money and give some of it to Crazy Cora to buy grub with. The rest of us played poker for yore horse and saddle and guns. I won the horse and saddle and Zeke Fossett ended up with the guns. But he traded one of them to that storekeeper at Rock Crossin' for a new suit of clothes." Again Astin glanced at the .44 in Graben's hand, but did not venture to add anything more.

Graben glanced off in the direction of Crazy Cora's shack. "What was that shot I heard over that way?"

"That was Tobe," Astin said. "He shot Crazy Cora. She tried to use that scattergun on him and he killed her."

"Better for him to do it than me, I guess," Graben said as if to himself. "I never liked the idea of killing a woman, but she was overdue."

"I ain't got no argument with you there," Dub Astin said readily.

Graben's pale cold eyes shifted back to him, had never really ceased to watch him. "You're all overdue," he said. "That's what I want you to tell the others. Tell them they're all going to die. I know they'll be looking for me, but I'll also be looking for them, and I'll pick my own time and my own ground. After a few more of you die, the rest may take it into their heads to start running. But tell them it will just be a waste of time. There's nowhere any of you can go or hide that I won't find you sooner or later.

"And tell the Radner boys if they want to take a hand, it's fine by me. The more the merrier. But once I see them on my trail, I'll start looking for them too."

A look of scorn came into his blue eyes as he added, "Now trot on back and tell the others."

Dub Astin did just that, and he added, rubbing his sweaty palms on his trousers, "He didn't take my gun. Never even mentioned it. I think he was hopin' I'd go for it."

"He's got nerve, I'll give him that," Tobe Unger said, his hard bright eyes narrowed at something in his mind. Then he looked at Astin. "He have a rifle?"

"I didn't see one. Just that open-top Colt in his hand and them Russian pistols that stranger was wearin'. Oh, that reminds me. I don't know why none of us didn't notice it before, but them two looked so much alike they could of been brothers."

Zeke Fossett slowly nodded. "They did look a lot alike, now you mention it."

Tobe Unger looked sharply at Astin. "Graben say anything about y'all killin' that stranger?"

Astin shook his head. "No, but I got me a hunch he didn't say nothin' about it on purpose 'cause he didn't want to give us the satisfaction of knowin' we killed his brother."

Tobe Unger's big dark face creased in a sudden smile that startled the others, for it was a very rare occasion indeed when Tobe Unger smiled. But he did not let them in on his secret, whatever it was.

"What are we waitin' for?" Barney Kester asked. He was a beady-eyed, bowlegged little man, testy and impatient and given at times to strutting pomposity. "He's gettin' away while we stand here jawin'."

Tobe Unger's smile immediately reverted to the usual scowl. "I'll say when we start. He's expectin' us now and he'll be waitin' in them rocks to ambush us. We'll just set here a while and rest our horses and let him get careless and then we'll go after him when he ain't expectin' it.

"But in the meantime, Barney, since you're so anxious to show how brave you are, why don't you see if you can make it to the Radner place and tell them we need some fresh horses."

The little man swallowed and there was a look of fear in his eyes. "You mean by myself?"

Unger nodded. "I can't afford to lose more'n one more man, Barney, and you just volunteered. But if you're scared, you can circle around the long way and Graben might not even see you."

"I ain't scared," Barney Kester said weakly.

CHAPTER 3

Barney Kester rode cautiously along the narrow winding trail, his eyes darting fearfully at the rocks.

Tom Graben grinned faintly when he saw the small man coming, dwarfed by the big ugly horse he rode. Graben stayed down behind the rocks until Kester was a little way past him, and then he rose and leveled a gun at the little man's back and said, "Hold it, Shorty."

Barney Kester stopped the big horse in its tracks and darted a wild look over his shoulder, his right hand going toward his gun.

"Don't try it, Shorty. Not till you've run a little errand for me."

Kester stopped the movement toward his gun. But he said resentfully, "I ain't Shorty. You already killed Shorty."

"That's right," Graben said, the hard grin extending to the other side of his mouth. "I believe they call you Barney. Barney Kester, somebody said. How come they called the other one Shorty? He was taller than you."

The little man bristled. "I drawed my gun on Shorty when he said that. I made him take it back."

"Well, I ain't looking for no trouble, Shorty," Graben said, still grinning. "I could see right off you weren't a man to fool with. I just thought you might deliver a message for me, seeing as how you're headed toward the Radner place anyway."

Barney Kester no longer twisted his neck to keep an eye on Graben, but sat on his big horse looking disdainfully ahead. He was not scared of a grinning fool who hid in the rocks. He made an impatient gesture. "What's the message?"

"Tell the Radner boys they better stay out of it," Graben said, no longer grinning. "If I see them on my trail or riding with you boys, I might get the idea they're looking for me, and then I'll be looking for them."

"Anything else?" Barney Kester asked.

"That's all I've got to say," Graben told him. "But you boys better keep one thing in mind the next time one of you decides to ride out alone. I won't be needing any more messages delivered, and that means I won't be needing any more messenger boys."

"What's that supposed to mean?" the little man asked.

"You think about it on the way to the Radner place, Barney," Graben told him. "It might come to you."

Barney Kester shrugged. "Well, I guess I'll be goin', if you're done talkin'."

"Go right ahead, Barney. I'm done talking."

Kester kneed the big horse and rode on along the trail through the rocks at a walk and Tom Graben stood there and watched him go. Once or twice the little man's right hand strayed as if by accident toward the butt of his holstered gun and Graben waited, his hard mouth grim and twisted with scorn for fools who never learned. But Barney Kester was smart enough to leave his gun in the holster. He walked the big horse on through the rocks until he was out of sight, and then he urged the animal to a fast, jolting trot.

The trail wound around and over eroded boulder-strewn hills, past buttes and weird rock formations and along twisting ravines and through a maze of canyons until it came to the hidden, grass-floored canyon where the three Radner brothers had their log shack and pole corral and kept a sharp watch for strangers who might be looking for stolen horses.

Most of the horses grazing in the high-walled canyon had been stolen, or else stolen horses had been traded for them. The Radner brothers did not like to keep rustled stock in their possession any longer than they could help, for even here in this hidden, remote place, well over a hundred miles from the nearest law, they did not feel completely safe. Men like them could never afford to get careless or take anything for granted.

All three Radner brothers were black-haired, dark-skinned young men still in their twenties, not much above medium height but strong-ly built. It was likely that some Indian blood flowed in their veins. Mac, the middle one, seemed to be the leader of the trio, although they all worked quietly together as a team and did not try to order each other around. Mac and the youngest one, Ed, had thick bushy black mustaches. Hump, the oldest, had a great sweeping handlebar mustache that curved down over his chin on either side and added to the dour, gloomy aspect of his face. All three had black eyes and surly dispositions, and like a great many western men, they usually wore cheap store suits that were seldom changed or patched until replaced.

The three came out of the shack when Barney Kester rode up, but they remained silent, waiting for him to speak. Hump and Ed lounged to either side, leaving Mac standing before the small man on the horse, to do the talking if any was necessary. Barney, not invited, did not dismount.

"I come to tell y'all," he said, drawing a deep breath to steady his voice, "Tom Graben has come back and Tobe said y'all better watch out for him. He's already killed Tim and Shorty." Barney squared himself in the saddle. "But I rid' right by him, even talked to him as close as you are, and he didn't mess with me."

Hump and Ed glanced silently at Mac, but Mac kept his dark eyes on Barney Kester. "Then y'all never killed him over there that night," Mac said. "I had a feelin' he might still be alive."

"How was we to know?" Barney Kester asked. "In the dark he looked like he was dead, and after we put all them holes in him we figgered he *had* to be dead."

"Some men ain't easy to kill," Mac Radner said. "What did he say when you talked to him."

"He said y'all better stay out of it," Barney replied. "He said if he saw y'all on his trail or ridin' with us when we come after him, he'd be lookin' for you."

Mac Radner's black eyes glinted. "He did, huh?"

"That's what he told me." Barney Kester puffed himself up in a vain attempt to look like a bigger man. "Tobe already sent Dub Astin over here, but Dub never got through. Graben took back that buck-skin horse and sent Dub back on foot. Then Tobe sent me over here. I guess he knowed I could get through if anybody could. He wanted y'all to come back with me and bring some fresh horses and help us look for him. There must be about a million places around here a man could hide, but y'all know this country better than we do and I guess Tobe figgered if anybody could find Graben, it's you boys."

"It don't sound to me like he's tryin' all that hard not to be found," Hump Radner said with a grin that, on his face, was almost as startling as Tobe Unger's smile had been earlier.

"I guess I should of mentioned," Barney Kester said resentfully, "Graben got the drop on me from behind. That's the only reason I didn't kill the bastard."

Hump Radner's crooked grin remained but he made no further comment, and he would not have guessed he had just made a bitter enemy for life.

"Ya'll comin' with me or not?" Barney Kester asked stiffly. "I don't care whether you do or not, myself. I'm only askin' 'cause Tobe said to."

Mac Radner glanced at his brothers. "What do y'all think?"

Hump Radner merely shrugged, but Ed said darkly, "Things has been pretty dull around here lately."

"Hell, let's give them a hand," Mac said. "I've had a feelin' all along that one of them ranchers around Rock Crossin' sent him over here to find out if we had any of their horses. Huntin' that cold-eyed bastard down will be fun." Mac grinned at his younger brother. "Like you say, things has been dull around here lately."

The sun was beating down on the rocks when Barney Kester, accompanied by the three Radner brothers, rode back along the narrow trail with four extra horses on lead ropes. Barney had left his big animal to "fatten" on the rich grass of Radner Canyon and now rode a fresh mount. They rode single file, their eyes searching the rocks, but they did not see Tom Graben.

From high in the rocks he watched them with bleak eyes. He could have been waiting near the trail and blasted some of them from their saddles before they even saw him, but he let them pass. He was in no hurry.

He was not surprised that the Radners had ignored the warning he had sent them. It was about what he had expected. He had even expected them to show their defiance by riding boldly back along the same trail where he had stopped Barney Kester earlier. It was like a kind of dare, a kind of challenge, to be expected from such men.

It amused Graben a little to see that Barney Kester had let Mac Radner precede him back along the narrow trail, with little doubt hoping that if Graben opened up on them Mac would get it first, maybe giving Kester himself a chance to dive for cover among the rocks. Graben was tempted to fire a shot just to see what the little man would do, but he decided against it. He knew if he fired a shot now, even at the sky, the three Radners would be coming after him; and he wanted to give them a while longer to think things over and maybe change their minds. When he took them on, in addition to the Unger gang, he wanted to be satisfied in his own mind that it could not have been avoided. He still had a small hope that they might decide to stay out of it, but that hope was rapidly fading.

He watched them until they were out of sight over the last ridge above Crazy Cora's shack, and then he went down through the rocks to where he had left the buckskin and the blue roan. Mounting the roan and leading the tired buckskin, he headed for Rock Crossing, to get supplies and give the Radner boys a little more time to think about it. He had enemies enough without them.

He took his time, resting his horses along the way and keeping an eye on his back trail, and rode into the tiny settlement two days later. He got a drink in the only saloon, a shave in the only barbershop and then went to the only store. There he traded one of his saddles for a packsaddle and enough supplies to last two or three weeks. He also bought a few clothes, some shells for his handguns, and would have bought himself a rifle but the storekeeper had sold his last one a few days before.

As he was riding out of town, Graben met the last person he had wanted to run into.

Belle Hopkins reined in her flax-maned sorrel and looked at him out of her clear direct blue eyes. "So you came back?"

"Just to pick up supplies," he said. "I'm leaving again." Then he asked, to steer the talk away from himself, "How's things at the ranch?"

"Things are fine at the ranch," she said impatiently. "But everyone's been wondering what happened to you. It wasn't very considerate of you to just go off like that without a word to anyone."

He looked at her long red-gold hair and sighed. "I thought it would be best that way," he said, folding his hands on the saddle horn. "I never was much at goodbyes."

She noticed the blue roan and the buckskin, the packsaddle laden with supplies, the new clothes he was wearing, and the guns. "Looks like you're ready to start a war," she said. "What did you do to get all that stuff? Rob a bank?"

"That reminds me," he said, reaching for Frank's wallet. "How much do I owe you?"

Her freckled face reddened as if he had insulted her. "You don't owe me anything."

"I figger it comes to about two hundred dollars," he said, counting out the money. "And if you don't take it, somebody a lot less deserving will prob'ly end up with it."

"In that case, I guess I might as well take it," she said, accepting the money. "But I'd still like to know where you got it. There wasn't a penny in your pockets when we found you."

"You know better than to ask a question like that," he said quietly.

"I'll ask anything I want to," she said angrily. "I took care of you when you were more dead than alive and everyone thought you would die. I nursed you just like I did my own father before he died. I reckon that gives me certain rights."

"Yeah, I reckon it does," Graben said heavily. "I owe you more than I can ever pay. You saved my life. But it's still my life, and I'll live it my way or not at all."

She studied him for a long moment with her clear unblinking eyes. "I might have known you'd say something like that," she said. "Just who the hell are you anyway?"

"I told you my name," he said. "I'm Tom Graben."

"Who's Tom Graben?" she asked.

"Nobody who's likely to be mentioned in the history books," he said. "I doubt if there are a dozen people back along the trail who remember me, and a lot fewer than that who miss me."

"What were you doing over there so close the Unger hideout and the Radner place?" she asked. "I know you were seen in Rock Crossing a few days before we found you. Did the Flying W or one of the other ranchers send you over that way to look for stolen horses?"

Graben shook his head. "Nobody sent me. I was just passing through and stopped at the wrong waterhole to fill my canteen and eat a bite of grub. But since you're asking so many questions this late in the day, maybe you won't mind if I ask one. What were *you* doing over that way? You and your hands? Is that what you were doing? Looking for stolen horses?"

She readily nodded. "I would have told you a long time ago if you'd bothered to ask."

"I'm not in the habit of asking questions that ain't any of my business," he said. "But now I guess I might as well ask one more. Did you find your horses?"

She shook her head. "No, we found you instead. We decided to forget about the horses and try to get you out of those hills before you finished bleeding to death."

A wry smile twisted Graben's thin lips. "Well, it looks like you made it."

"Just barely," she said. "To tell you the truth, I never thought you'd make it. How you pulled through I'll never know. And I sure never expected to see you back on your feet as soon as you were."

"I had a good nurse," he said, meeting her glance.

She blinked once, which was unusual for her. Those wide, clear blue eyes almost never blinked or shifted away even for a moment. "I don't think I'd want to go through that again," she told him. "The next time you get yourself all shot up, you'll have to find yourself another nurse."

"I'll keep that in mind," he said.

She again glanced at his guns. "You don't need three pistols to shoot rabbits," she said. "So I don't guess I have to ask where you're headed now."

"No, I don't guess you do."

She studied him silently a moment. And then she asked, "Like some help?"

"No, it's my fight." He smiled bleakly. "And I wouldn't want to share those boys with anyone. Not even you, Belle. Especially you."

"Well, don't let me keep you from your fun, Graben," she said, and started to ride past him. Then she stopped and gave him a searching look. "Forget what I said a minute ago," she said. "If you get shot up again, I'll do whatever I can for you."

He sighed. "Thanks, Belle. I appreciate it."

"I'd do the same for anyone," she told him, and rode on into town without looking back.

After a moment Tom Graben rode on in the opposite direction, heading back the way he had come.

CHAPTER 4

On the return trip, Graben avoided his previous route in order to avoid the men who were probably on his trail. As he had said, he would pick his own time and ground, and he did not want to run into all of them in the open. He might get a few of them but the others would get him, and he did not want it to work out that way. He wanted to get all of them before they got him.

Two days later he was back in his cave in the badlands. He had seen no one since leaving Rock Crossing, except for Belle Hopkins just outside of town. Now he was glad he had seen her and given her the two hundred dollars. He doubted if he would ever see her again and he felt better knowing he had paid his debt to her the only way he could. It did not make up for all she had done for him, a total stranger when they had found him shot full of holes and more dead than alive, but it was all he could do, being the kind of man he was.

Losing his only brother had not changed the kind of man Tom Graben was, although it had made him deeply regret being the way he was. He knew he had really lost Frank a long time ago because of his unyielding pride and incurable aloofness, his inability to get close to anyone. Even his own brother.

He had not been able to get close to Belle Hopkins either, and he knew it was not her fault but his. During his long months of recovery at the Hopkins ranch he had thought about her a lot, but had never said more than a few words to her at a time and had never spoken at all of what he felt inside. And then, when he was well enough, he had left without saying goodbye or even telling her that he was going.

No, it was not much of a way to show his gratitude for all she had done for him. But he was Tom Graben and he could not seem to change. He could not be like other men—perhaps because, deep down, he had no wish to be like them.

But soon it would not matter to anyone what kind of man he was, or had been. For Tom Graben would soon be dead. There was not one chance in a hundred that he would come out of this fight alive.

Just as well, perhaps. He could see no future for a man like him in the world that other men were so busy creating. It was to get away from that growing world that he had come here in the first place, to this godforsaken country where the past might last a while longer because the people who were creating the future were busy elsewhere.

So here in this remote, forgotten place, Tom Graben would live out his last few hours or days or weeks, and here he would die. Here he would make his last stand, against men who, like himself, belonged to a past that was almost gone.

After dark he picketed his horses in a nearby ravine where there was a little poor grass and an intermittent trickle of bad-tasting water. It was the best he could do for his animals. The sack of grain he had brought back would have to be conserved as long as possible.

Then he walked to the base of the cliff where he had buried Frank and sat down on a rock near the grave. He sat there without moving and in the moonlight he looked like a projection of the rock he was sitting on. He sat there for over an hour thinking about himself and Frank growing up on that bleak farm in Missouri. It might have helped if he could have cried, but he could not cry. He just felt lost and empty inside and sort of numb. He was the only one left now of that family and it looked like he was running out of time himself.

After a while he found himself remembering the way those four men had shot into Frank at close range when he was almost dead already, and a bitter rage engulfed him. He got to his feet and started back for the cave, telling himself he would never pass up another chance to kill Dub Astin, or any of the others.

He was almost back to the cave when he discovered that the open-top Colt was not in his waistband. He had probably taken it out without thinking and laid it down beside him on the rock. He often did that when he sat down, for the sake of comfort, but he had never gone off and left it anywhere before. The very thought of going back after the gun made him realize how tired he was, but he did not want to leave the gun there overnight. So he went back and felt on the rock for the gun. He ran his hand all over the top of the rock even though he should have been able to see the gun if it was there, even in the shadows at the base of the cliff. Then he bent down and felt along the ground around the rock, thinking the gun might have fallen off. But the gun was gone!

Somebody had been here since he had left, and might still be around somewhere.

He swept the area with a rapid glance and backed up against the face of the cliff, drawing one of the Smith & Wesson pistols. He did not cock the gun but kept his thumb ready on the hammer while his eyes continued to search the shadows and rocks where anyone might hide. But he saw no one and heard no sound, and a strange creepy feeling came over him.

Something ain't right here, he thought. He did not know just what he meant by that, but he knew something was not right and it scared him.

He did not believe anyone had been here since he had left. But what had happened to the gun? Could he have left it somewhere else and only thought he had left it here? Perhaps when he got back to the cave he would find it there.

When he entered the dark cave a little later the strange feeling came over him again. His scalp prickled, there was a strange ringing in his ears, and a chill went down his spine.

More frightened than he had been in a long time, he stepped quickly to one side, gripping one of Frank's pistols in his hand, his eyes searching the darkness of the cave. But somehow he knew there was no one in the cave, although a moment before he had had the odd feeling that someone walked past him, leaving as he came in.

Tom Graben had always considered himself the sanest man in the world, but now he almost wondered if he might be losing his mind.

He lay down in the dark cave and tried to sleep. Toward morning he finally dozed off and dreamed that Frank was standing in the cave in his blood-spattered black clothes gazing down at him through glittering gray eyes. He woke up in a cold sweat and did not try to go back to sleep.

When it was light enough he thoroughly searched the cave but failed to find the missing gun. He went back to Frank's grave to look for it again there in the daylight, but it was not there either.

Looking at the grave, he got the odd notion that some of the rocks were not as he had arranged them. But he told himself it was just his imagination. After all, he had not seen the grave before in the daylight, and nothing looked quite the same at night.

When he went to the ravine to bring in the horses, there was another surprise in store for him.

The blue roan was gone.

Graben saddled the buckskin and set out on the blue roan's trail. He soon lost the tracks on the hard rocky ground, but not before he was convinced that the horse had been ridden. No horse that had pulled its picket pin would have selected the roan's route over the most difficult terrain, as if deliberately trying to leave no trail that could be followed.

On his way back to the cave, he suddenly thought about the old saddle he had discarded and hidden behind some rocks and brush near Frank's grave when he had turned his crowbait horse loose. On a hunch, he decided to see if the saddle was still there.

It wasn't.

And then, just when Tom Graben was convinced that he had lost his mind, he found a small boot track that explained everything. Or almost everything.

Later, from the rocks on the ridge above Crazy Cora's old shack, he kept watch for a while. He saw no one, but there were two horses in the corral. One of them had probably belonged to Crazy Cora, but the other suggested that someone might have stayed behind to keep an eye on the place when the others took up Graben's trail.

He saw smoke rising from the chimney. So someone was down there, and the fact that the smoke was coming from the chimney and not the stovepipe indicated that it was a man who was unused to cooking on a stove. Graben was tempted to pay whoever it was a little visit, but for the moment he had lost interest in the Unger gang. He had even lost interest, temporarily, in revenge.

Returning to the cave, he made a meal of hardtack and jerky and washed it down with a little water from his canteen. He kept thinking about the missing pistol. He had been handling guns all his life, or at least the biggest part of it, and this was the first time he had ever lost or misplaced one.

The open-top Colt of 1872 was the first cartridge revolver brought out by the company, appearing well over a year before the Peacemaker. It was called an open-top Colt because there was no strap over the cylinder. Some of them had the large Army stock; others, like the Peacemaker, had the slightly smaller Navy stock which enhanced the gun's appearance. The one Graben had lost had a Navy stock, a long barrel, and weighed over two pounds. A good-sized weapon. It was hard to believe he had failed to miss its weight immediately although, it was true, he was so accustomed to the gun in his waistband that he rarely noticed it until he sat down. Then, if he was by himself, he often took it out and laid it aside, automatically reaching for it when he started to rise again, or when something alerted him to danger. That was the gun he always reached for in an emergency, whether it was in his waistband, in his lap, or on the ground beside him. It was his constant companion, and when he had seen it in the store at Rock Crossing he had recognized it even before he had noticed the little scratch on the walnut stock, picked up in some forgotten encounter with thorny brush. Amazed at his luck in finding an old friend, he had not complained about paying out most of what money he had left after buying the plug horse at the stable and leaving the Hopkins horse to be picked up by someone from the ranch where he had stayed for five months and worked most of the last two, though he had accepted pay for only one month and even that reluctantly, because he needed an outfit of some kind.

Now apparently he had laid the gun down somewhere and left it there. But where?

He thought about the small boot track he had seen near the grave. He had a pretty good idea who had made the track, though he could not yet be sure. In any case, his hideout was no longer much of a secret, or would not remain so for long.

Whoever it was might even have been inside the cave. But none of his stuff seemed to be missing, except for the pistol, which might or might not have been left here. Even during the day it was too dark in the cave to make an adequate search for tracks, and the ground outside the cave was so hard and rocky a draft horse could have trotted by without leaving any sign.

Well, Frank, it looks like I've already lost my gun and your horse, he thought. I guess it was to be expected, the way our luck's been going lately. It was a bad day for both of us when we first rode into this country, and I reckon you'd feel the same way, if you could feel anything.

He remembered the strange chill that had come over him a couple of times. He had never believed in ghosts or spirits or anything like that, and still didn't, but now he could almost understand why some people did believe in such things, and why they feared the dead even if they had not feared the same people when they were alive.

And some things had gone on around here lately that he still did not have all the answers to. But maybe he would know more about that when he located the owner of that small boot.

The cave was in the steep side of a mesa. He had never gone far in the West without seeing a mesa of some kind. This one was rather small, no more than half a mile across at the widest point. But Graben had no idea what it was like up on top. He had found no trail up the steep wall. There probably was some sort of trail, but he had not yet found it.

Frank's grave was at the foot of the mesa, not far from the cave and at a point where the mesa wall curved inward, forming an L. Up on the rim a few stunted cedars grew, none of them taller than a man on a horse.

Shortly after dark, Graben, playing a hunch, hid in the brush and rocks near Frank's grave where he could watch the rim without being seen. From here he could also keep an eye on the rocks around the grave, but mostly he watched the rim.

He saw nothing for what seemed a long time and he became cramped and stiff and a chill seeped into his bones. The day had been hot but after dark a cold wind had sprung up, tossing the dark twisted cedars on the rim.

Suddenly he saw something move up there and then a rider appeared on a dark horse and sat there motionless on the rim, looking out over the broken land below. The rider was starkly outlined against the sky and in the moonlight Graben could see that it was a girl with long pale hair blowing in the wind.

She was there for only a few minutes, then horse and rider turned back from the rim and disappeared.

Chapter 5

Tom Graben remained where he was, thinking about what he had just seen. He discovered that he was gripping one of Frank's Russian pistols in his hand, and he glanced curiously down at the gun that many experts considered the best-balanced and most beautifully made handgun ever built. Yet it looked strange and felt strange in the hand of a man who had carried a Colt all his life.

But then, everything about this place was beginning to seem strange and unreal, and Graben was beginning to have strange thoughts about his dead brother whom he had not seen in over ten years. What sort of man had Frank become? What had he been doing all those years? Where had he gotten all that money. Five hundred dollars was more than most men managed to save in a lifetime.

And who was that tall, slender, pale-haired girl he had just seen up on the rim?

Graben thought he knew who she was. If he was not mistaken, he had seen her once before, the night he had stopped at Crazy Cora's place. She could not have been much over seventeen then, yet he had seen very few women with a figure like hers. And though she had not said much, she had not seemed at all crazy like her mother. A little strange perhaps, but not crazy.

Wondering if she would come down here again, Graben decided to wait where he was.

After a while he heard a horse approaching along the foot of the mesa at a walk, the sound of the shod hoofs on the rocky ground plainly audible. But from where he was he could not see the horse or its rider and he watched and waited for them to come on around into view. Then the sound stopped and he heard nothing else for a long time, saw nothing.

Then the pale-haired girl appeared again, as suddenly and silently as she had appeared up on the rim. Only this time she was down below, not far from Graben, and on foot, slipping along without a sound. She was keeping close to the mesa wall and looking back over her shoulder as if she were being followed.

And she was. The dark figure of a man loomed into view and his boots clattered on the rocks as he ran after the girl. She gave a little cry and stretched her long legs in flight, but almost immediately tripped on something and sprawled on her face. The man was upon her at once and there was a fierce struggle, with the outcome by no means certain. The silent girl fought like a wildcat and the man grunted in pain and rage and brought up his gun to bring it down on her blond head.

That was when Graben rose to his feet and seeing him, the man shoved the girl away from him with his left hand and at the same time brought the gun in his right down to bear on Graben. The Russian barked and the man whined and crumpled to the ground.

The girl looked at Graben and started to run again.

"Hold it," he said sharply as he strode forward, and something in his voice, or perhaps the gun in his hand, made her obey him. She stood and watched in uneasy silence as he stepped up and turned the man over with the toe of his boot. Satisfied that the man was dead, he glanced at her and asked, "Know him?"

She slowly nodded, watching him. "It's that no-account Clyde Picker. He must have followed me."

"What are you doing here?" Graben asked, holstering his gun.

"What are *you* doin' here?" she retorted.

"I asked first."

She shrugged, amazingly calm after what she had just experienced. Her hands were on her hips, her elbows crooked out from her sides. She wore tight Levi's and a man's shirt, but no coat in spite of the cold wind. She was a tall lean girl, but nicely rounded in all the right places. In the moonlight her face seemed rather pale, but that night at Crazy Cora's he had noticed that it was tanned to a golden brown, as if she spent a lot of time outdoors in the sun and wind, which might also have bleached her long blond hair. She reminded him of a beautiful wild pony he had once seen, a golden pony with a flowing white mane.

"I was tryin' to get away from him," she said, nodding at the man on the ground. "Tobe Unger and them left me at Turley's and Tobe told me to stay there. But I wanted to see my mama so I come back home, but there wasn't anyone there but Clyde and he said she'd been shot. He said Tom Graben shot her. But I didn't believe him. I figgered it was one of them and I finally got the truth out of him. He said he'd tell me a secret if I'd promise not to tell Tobe and if I'd be nice to him. So I promised and he told me it was Tobe who shot her and then he said he wanted his reward and he came at me and I hit him with a skillet and got out of there. But he staggered outside as I was tryin' to get me a horse out of the corral, and I headed for the rocks on foot. I outran him and hid in the rocks until it was dark and then I remembered this place and came here. I think I'm the only one who knows about the trail up to the top and I figgered I'd be safe up there.

"Then last night I was standin' up there on the rim thinking about jumpin' off. I was goin' to kill myself because I didn't have nothin' to live for. Then I saw you sittin' down here on that rock over there and I got so scared I forgot all about killin' myself. Then you left and later I saw you come back and it looked like you were lookin' for somethin', but it didn't look like you found it. I got to wonderin' what it was and after you left the next time I decided to come down here and see if I could find it. I thought it might be money. But all I found was an old saddle over there in the brush. I started just to leave it, but then I got to thinkin' maybe I could steal a horse from you. So I went lookin' in the direction you'd gone and I found them two horses in that ravine. I took the dark one because that buckskin looks like the one Dub Astin's been ridin' and I knew he'd kill me if he caught me on that horse. Anyway, I took the roan and the saddle and tried not to leave no trail you could follow. That's a trick I learned from Tobe and them."

"Did Tobe and them teach you to steal too?" Graben asked.

She shrugged as if bored. "I figgered anybody hidin' out in a place like this was a thief anyway and maybe worse, and I didn't see anything wrong with stealin' from a thief. And I know that buckskin don't belong to you. Not unless you're Tom Graben." She looked up at him. "Are you Tom Graben?"

"That's right," he said. "And the buckskin belongs to me. So does that blue roan you stole. Where did you leave him?"

She pointed with her chin, like an Indian. "Back around there a piece. I wasn't so sure you hadn't come back to look for whatever you were lookin' for last night. And it looks like I was right. What were you lookin' for anyway?"

"A gun I thought I left on that rock," Graben told her. "You sure you didn't find it?"

She shook her head. "Believe me, if I had a gun I would have used it on Clyde Picker."

"Somehow I believe you would have," Graben said dryly. Then he asked, "How many people besides you and him know about this place?"

"I didn't even know he knew about it," she said. "I don't know how he found me, especially in the dark. But maybe he wasn't lookin' for me. Maybe he was looking for you."

"That's possible, I guess," Graben admitted.

"Are you stayin' around there in that old cave?" she asked.

Graben nodded. He saw no point in denying it.

"That's what I figgered," she said. "I thought about goin' there myself, but I figgered they'd soon find me there. And I'm afraid Tobe will kill me too, just like he did my mama. He'll be afraid I'll try to get him hung for it, or kill him myself the first chance I get. And he could be right. I thought I liked him before I ran off with him, but after I found out what he was really like I couldn't stand his guts. I would have come back home before now but he wouldn't let me, and he said he'd kill me if I ever tried to run off. He'll do it too. That's why I'm afraid to go back to the house. I'm afraid they'll come back and find me there."

Then she looked at Graben and asked, "You got anything to eat? I'm starvin'."

"First help me pile some rocks over him," Graben said, nodding at the dead Picker. "I don't want the buzzards bringing Tobe Unger and the others over this way."

They rolled the dead man into a gully and piled rocks on top of him.

"I didn't even think to see if he had any money on him," the girl said. "He prob'ly didn't. That bunch is the brokest outlaws I ever heard of. Tobe used to try to borrow back the money he give Mama to buy groceries with, sometimes after we'd already eaten the groceries and she was plannin' to ask him for some more. It's enough to make a person turn honest. But they're all too lazy to work. I guess that's why they became outlaws in the first place."

Graben glanced at her and grinned. "Did I hear someone call you Gibby that night? Or was it Gabby?"

Her white teeth flashed in a brief smile. "It's Gibby. Maybe it should be Gabby. But I usually don't have much to say. I don't know why I'm talkin' so much tonight. To keep from being scared, I guess."

"Are you scared of me?" Graben asked in surprise.

"A little, I guess," she said. "After what happened to you that night, I reckon you'll try to get even with somebody. But that wasn't none of my doing. If I'd known they were goin' to do that, I would of tried to warn you somehow."

"I'm surprised you didn't remember me."

"You mean tonight? I thought that was you, but I couldn't tell for sure in the dark."

"I didn't have any trouble recognizing you," Graben said. "That long blond hair." Then he asked, "How old are you?"

"Almost eighteen." She glanced at him. "I bet you thought I was older, didn't you? Men usually think I'm quite a bit older than I am. That's one reason I ran off with Tobe Unger. I was beginnin' to feel like an old maid and them outlaws were about the only men who ever came around. There wasn't much to choose from."

She laid a rock on the grave and sat down with a weary sigh. "God, I'm tired. Ain't that enough rocks?"

"Yeah, that should about do it," Graben said. He dusted off his hands and picked up the shell belt and holstered gun he had taken from the dead man. "Let's see if we can find that blue roan and Picker's horse and then go round up something to eat."

"That reminds me of something," Gibby Tate said as they went to get the horses. "Would you like to know how I got back from Turley's?"

"I can see I'm going to, whether I like it or not."

"When I was about ten miles from home my horse stepped in a hole and broke its leg," she said. "I didn't know what I was gonna do. I didn't even have a gun to shoot it with. Then about that time a man rode up on a dark bay and I asked him if he'd put my horse out of its misery. He didn't say anything. He just looked at me, then looked at the horse and shot it. I didn't see him draw his gun. He looked at the horse for a minute to make sure it was dead and then put his gun back in the holster and looked at me, sort of frownin' like he didn't know what to do about me.

"I told him where I was headed and asked if I could ride the rest of the way with him. He said he didn't think his horse would mind if I didn't. Said it sort of solemn like. I think that's about the only thing he said till we got in sight of our old shack, and then he said he guessed that was about as far as he should go, if I wouldn't mind walkin' the rest of the way. I'd been talkin' the whole ten miles, like now, and told him all about Tobe and them bein' outlaws and all, and I guess that's why he didn't want to go any closer. Anyway, I got down and he rode off and I ain't seen him since."

"You must have told him what happened to me over there that night."

"No, I didn't even mention that. I don't guess I had to, after all the rest I told him. I told him I was afraid Tobe would kill me if he came back and found me there. I was sort of hopin' he would offer to stay and protect me or something. I'd seen how he could handle a gun. But he never said a word. He probably thought I was just jokin' or exaggeratin' or something."

"What did that fellow look like?" Graben asked, idly curious, while his eyes searched the brush and rocks for Picker's horse.

"He was about your size I guess. Maybe not quite as tall, but close to it. Sort of a handsome fellow, except he never smiled. Had dark brown hair with a sort of copper shine to it and dark gray eyes. And he was dressed in black. Black hat, shirt, pants, everything."

Graben looked at her with interest. "You sure his eyes were dark gray? They couldn't have been light gray?"

"No, they were dark gray, almost black," she said. "Why? Does that sound like someone you know?"

"No, but I knew a man who wore black clothes like that. He was my brother."

"Was?"

"He's dead now. Some of your friends killed him."

"They ain't my friends," she told him. "I've got so I can't stand any of them. But I despise Tobe Unger more than any of the others. I don't know how they put up with him. It's just about impossible to be around that man very much of the time—and I had to be around him *all* of the time. Never let me out of his sight. He was afraid to leave me behind, so he took me with him everywhere he went—until he started back this way, the very place he knew I wanted so bad to go. Then he left me behind. It was just like him to pull a stunt like that. I think he did it mainly just to spite me, because he knew how bad I wanted to see my mama. Then the bastard killed her, and now I won't ever get to see her again."

Graben remembered the way Frank's back had looked when Crazy Cora had put all that buckshot in him. In his opinion, the old hellcat had richly deserved to die. But he did not say anything.

Later, back in the cave, he asked, "What's it like up on top."

"Rocks," Gibby Tate said, the word dodging past the beans in her mouth. She seemed to be doing her best to eat up all the grub he had packed in from Rock Crossing, and his attempt to distract her was not having the desired effect. She kept right on shoveling it in while she talked. "Rocks everywhere, like down here. Stunted cedars and a few good-sized mesquite trees. But more grass than you'd expect."

"Water?"

She was silent until she had finished that plate of beans. Then she looked wistfully at the nearly empty pot, but set the tin plate down and wiped her mouth. "You won't believe it," she said, "But there's a waterhole up there. Don't ask me where it comes from, but it's up there. I never meant to tell anyone. It's been my secret since I found it four or five years ago. I used to go up there to get away from everyone and be by myself."

"What about the Radners? Do they know about it?"

She shook her head. "I ain't seen any sign that there's ever been anyone up there except me. I don't think anyone else knows how to get up there."

"The trail must not be too bad, if you got up there with a horse."

"It's a goat trail," she said. "I just knew me and that horse both would splatter on the rocks below. But I didn't figger I had much to lose. If Tobe Unger finds me he'll kill me, and I don't know of any place except up on that mesa where he won't find me."

"You really think he'll try to kill you?" Graben asked.

She slowly nodded, her eyes tragic. "Yes, I really do."

Graben watched her in silence, and she glanced at the dying fire. "He might not, if he thought I'd stay with him and never try to run off or tell anyone about all the things he's done. But there's no way I'm goin' to live with that man after he killed my mama. Maybe she was a little crazy like everyone said, but that was more puttin' on than anything else. She was as sane as anyone when she wanted to be. And who can blame her for not havin' no use for men, after the way they treated her? All any of them ever did was use her, and after they got what they wanted they went off and left her to get by as best she could till they took a notion to come back and put up on her again for a while. And the one she married was just as bad as the rest. He went off and left her with a kid to raise by herself.

"And if she tried to use that shotgun on Tobe, like Clyde Picker said she did, it was only because she knew he'd treat me the way he treated her. After he got tired of me, he'd go off and leave me to get by any way I could. Or maybe even kill me if he thought I'd tell anyone about some of the things he's done."

After studying her in silence a while, Graben asked, "You feel the same way about men as your mother did?"

She sat gazing into the fire with her lips twisted in an expression of bitter resentment. But whether it was him she resented, or men in general, he could not tell. "I don't like the way men treated her," she said. "And I don't like the way Tobe Unger has treated me. After he kept after me the way he did to go off with him. All the fun we could have. All the good times. Hah! I was a lot happier and had a lot more fun before I left home than I ever did with him. The bastard never even bothered to marry me, but he wouldn't let me leave either."

Graben's lips twisted in a crooked grin. "I'm beginning to think I won't have to kill Unger. Just give you a gun when I see him, and get back out of the way."

CHAPTER 6

In the years to come there were many conflicting accounts of what happened up on the mesa that night. Tom Graben himself never told anyone, but around the turn of the century a woman claiming to be Gibby Tate gave the following account. At the time her story was generally discredited because it was thought that Gibby Tate had been dead for almost twenty years.

But according to this mysterious woman with long blond hair, still under forty at the time she told her story and still very attractive, this is what happened.

It was the girl who suggested that they move up on the mesa while it was dark, lest they be seen in the daylight.

"Think we'll have any trouble on the cliff?" Graben asked.

"It was dark when I came down," she reminded him.

Graben shrugged. He was game if she was.

So they saddled up and using the dead Picker's horse for a pack animal they headed for the secret trail, keeping to the shadows along the base of the cliff.

When they reached the spot where they had buried Picker, Graben drew rein and looked silently toward the rocks at the base of the cliff. After a moment he dismounted and walked over to the rocks and the girl saw him stop near the rock on which he had sat for a while the previous night. He stood there for a few minutes and then he came back and got back into his saddle.

"Were you looking for that gun again?" she asked.

Graben did not answer. He sat motionless in his saddle looking toward the rocks.

"Hey," she said, "are you all right?"

"I had a strange feeling someone was trying to tell me something," he said. "Or warn me about something. I ain't sure what it is, but something ain't right around here." For a moment he looked at the girl as if she might be the cause of something not being right. Then he said, "Let's get out of here."

They rode on around the foot of the mesa until the girl pointed. She led the way into a gap in the mesa wall that at first appeared to be filled with boulders and brush. But she found a narrow trail through the rocks and Graben followed her, leading the packhorse. A moment later they began the climb up the steep slope along what appeared to be a game trail. The trail angled and looped so that it was not as steep as might have been expected, and the main danger was slipping off it in the dark, not tumbling back down it.

But they made it to the top and Graben looked out across relatively flat ground strewn with boulders and dotted with stunted black cedars writhing in the wind that moaned through the rocks. In the moonlight there was something dismal and eerie about the place that made him uneasy.

"Where's that waterhole you mentioned?" he asked, looking toward a dark mesquite thicket where a few full-sized trees towered over the lower brush.

She pointed. "Over there." As they picked their way through the rocks in that direction, she added, "It's not actually a waterhole. Just some rainwater in a rock tank. But it should last a while."

When they reached the spot and dismounted, Graben saw that there was only a few inches of water in the bottom of a shallow depression floored with rock. He looked at the girl and scowled. "There ain't enough water here to last us and three horses more than a few days."

"I think there's another tank on the other side of that rock," she said, pointing. "But I didn't check to see if there was any water in it."

Graben went toward the rock, and Crazy Cora Tate rose from behind it with a shrieking scream and began blazing away at him with a big pistol.

Rattled, Graben hit the ground, jerked out a gun and fired back at the screeching apparition. There was an unearthly howl as Crazy

Cora dropped her gun, clutched at her middle with both hands and fell forward over the rock.

"Mama!" Gibby Tate screamed and ran past Graben to ease the old woman off the rock to the ground and kneel beside her. She put an ear to the old woman's chest to listen. A cry of anguish was torn from her, and then she began feeling about on the ground.

Graben stepped forward as she lifted the gun and kicked it out of her hand. He slapped her hard with his left hand and she fell with a grunt.

She started back up as if to fight him. Then, still on her knees, she doubled over crying and holding her stomach with both hands as if that was where he had hit her.

Graben picked up the open-top Colt and showed it to her. "How did she happen to have this?" he asked harshly. "No, don't tell me. Let me guess. You found it down there on that rock where I left it, and you brought it up here and gave it to her. Then you led me up here knowing she was waiting to kill me. You and her cooked it up between you. You set me up!"

"She was my mama!" the girl cried. "They didn't even bury her, they just took her off and dumped her, like they did you! I followed their tracks to see where they took her and found her still alive, and I brought her up here where I didn't think they'd find her. I did what I could for her, but I knew I had to get her out of here and find a doctor, and to do that I had to have horses and money. I knew you had horses and I figgered you might have money too—and when it came to a choice between you and her, I'd pick her any day!"

Graben shook his head, quietly cussing his own stupidity. "I never seem to learn. I stop by her place and get shot all to hell, she fills my brother's back full of buckshot when he shows up, then I let her whelp lead me into her range again." He glanced at the dead woman and added, "But the Unger bunch don't seem to learn very fast either. If you aim to shoot somebody it's a good idea to make sure they're dead."

"You can do what you want to me," Gibby Tate said, sobbing. "She was my mama. I had to do whatever I could for her."

Graben glanced at her with cold eyes. "It looks like I'm the one who killed her after all," he said bitterly. "Now I guess you'll try to get even with me for that. You already tried it once."

"I sort of lost my head," she said meekly.

"That seems to run in the family," Graben told her, as he punched the empty shells from the open-top Colt and began reloading.

The girl looked at him with hatred in her eyes, but did not say anything. She had quit crying.

"What you aim to do with her?" Graben asked, gesturing at the still body of Crazy Cora Tate. It had been on the tip of his tongue to say "that" instead of "her," but he caught himself in time.

The girl glanced at her dead mother and swallowed. "I guess I'll have to bury her somehow." She looked out across the windy mesa. "And I guess up here somewhere is as good a place as any. I'd just as soon Tobe and them don't know where the grave is."

"Pick your spot and I'll help you carry her," Graben said, thrusting the Colt in his waistband.

Gibby looked about and then pointed. "Over near that big mesquite looks like a good place. I sit there a lot when I come up here, and I'd like to have the grave there where I can sit near it."

In helping the girl carry her mother to the mesquite, Graben checked the pulse of the old murderess to make sure she really was dead. He did not want to spend the rest of his life wondering if Crazy Cora Tate was waiting behind every rock to kill him. But she seemed to be dead this time.

Graben nodded toward a little depression near the mesquite and that was where they put her.

"I'll do the rest," Gibby Tate said coldly.

Graben shrugged and silently withdrew. While he stripped the gear from the horses and let them drink a little of the water in the natural tank, he watched her break twigs from nearby cedars and place them on her mother. Then she began piling rocks on the layer of cedar twigs and branches, starting at her mother's feet and working toward the head.

As Graben was picketing the horses on the best grass he could find near the tank, he heard a low nicker and looked up to see the gaunt nag he had turned loose, standing about fifty yards away and looking toward him. The poor animal's head hung low and every rib seemed to show in the moonlight.

Exclaiming softly in surprise, Graben looked around and saw Gibby Tate returning from the mound of rocks near the big mesquite. Gesturing toward the nag, he asked, "How did you manage to get *him* up here."

"I found him grazing down below," she said. "That's how I got Mama up here. I couldn't have carried her."

"It's a wonder he didn't fall on that cliff," Graben said. "I didn't think he'd ever get me here from Rock Crossing."

"And you just turned him loose to starve?" the girl said.

Graben shrugged. "I figgered he'd find enough grass and water to get by on. And I figgered if I needed him again he wouldn't be hard to find. But I wouldn't have thought to look for him up here."

"What do you intend to do with him now?" she asked.

"He's yours now," Graben told her. "Him and Picker's sorrel too for all I care. I've got all the horses I need."

After a silent moment she folded her arms and asked, "What you aim to do about me?"

"Keep an eye on you tonight," he said. "After that you're on your own."

"What do you mean?"

"I mean," he said, "you and I are parting company at first light. I can't keep an eye on you every minute of the time and I don't intend to try."

"You mean you don't trust me." It didn't sound like a question.

Graben nodded. "You're getting warm."

He rolled up in his blankets near the tank, using his saddle for a pillow, and watched Gibby Tate from under his pulled-down hat brim. She bedded down about twenty feet away where she could see the mound of rocks near the edge of the small mesquite thicket, which seemed in the wrong place, surrounded by and mixed with the stunted cedars.

"God, I feel awful," she said after a while. "Maybe she wasn't any good in some ways, but she was all I had."

"She filled my brother's back full of buckshot," Graben said. "Did Picker tell you that?"

"He said something about it. But she must have had a reason."

"She probably did have," he said bitterly. "About the same reason she had for trying to kill me. She thought he might have money."

"That wasn't her idea," the girl said. "She didn't know anything about you till I told her."

"Then it was your idea?" Graben asked.

"I didn't want to do it," she said. "Especially after you saved me from Clyde Picker. But I kept thinkin' about her up here with that bullet in her, and I knew if I didn't soon get her to a doctor she'd die. I was afraid that horse you turned loose would drop dead on us, so I needed your other horse, and any money you had to pay the doctor.

I know how that must sound to you, but all I could think of was my mama up here bleedin' to death and countin' on me to save her."

"Of course it never occurred to you to ask for help instead of plotting to murder me," Graben said dryly.

"I had a pretty good idea who you were," she said, "and I didn't believe you'd go to much trouble to help Crazy Cora Tate out. And I didn't believe for a minute that you'd loan us your horses, much less any money to pay a doctor with, and I was afraid he might not try very hard to save her life unless he knew he was going to get paid for it."

"Aren't you forgetting something?" Graben asked. "Your friends took all my money the night they shot me."

"That was five or six months ago," she said. "I thought you might have got hold of some more since then. And you must have, or you wouldn't of bought all that stuff you've got."

Graben was silent.

"Was I right?" she asked.

"The money belonged to my brother," Graben said. "If Crazy Cora and those others hadn't killed him, I'd be as broke as you are. Since that night they tried to kill me, I've earned thirty dollars and spent all of it on that old plug horse and a cheap outfit."

"Well, it don't matter now," Gibby Tate said. "Our plan didn't work. You've still got your money and your horses, and you know what you can do with them."

She turned over on her side with her back to him and lay facing the other way.

Graben thought of several things he was tempted to tell her, but he knew it would do no good, so he remained silent, watching her from under his hat brim. It was going to be a long night, for he didn't dare go to sleep. But after the night was over he would be rid of her.

He thought of Belle Hopkins. Now there was a woman a man could count on, and he knew he would always hate the man Belle eventually married, even if he never saw the man. Unless, of course, the man happened to be Tom Graben. But there was not much chance of that. He had nothing to offer her, even if he got out of this fight alive.

About an hour later, when it was getting harder and harder for him to hold his eyes open, the old horse he had turned loose came up to the tank and tried to drink it dry.

"Hey, get away from there!" Graben said, and got up to scare the greedy beast away.

"Oh, leave that poor old horse alone," Gibby Tate said. "He's probably thirsty."

"He'll be a lot thirstier if he don't save some of that water for later," Graben said. He got the old horse turned away from the tank and sent him on his way with a slap on his bony rump. Then Graben returned to his blankets, saying, "You better try to get some sleep. You may need it tomorrow."

"How can I go to sleep with you layin' over there watchin' me like a hawk?" she asked resentfully.

"How did you know I was watching you?"

"I can feel it," she said. "And I know men. They're always watchin' me. What have you got on your mind, anyway?"

"Not that," he said. "If you really want to know what I've got on my mind, I've been thinking how nice it will be to get you off my hands, so I can get some sleep."

She raised up on one elbow and looked at him. "You ain't got much use for us Tates, have you, Graben?" When he did not answer at once, she said, "If you feel that way, I'd just as soon leave tonight."

"I'd just as soon you didn't," he told her. "The mood you're in, you might do something we'll both regret."

"Like what?"

"Like try to find the Unger bunch and tell them where I am."

"I already told you how I feel about Tobe Unger," she said. "I hate that man more than I've ever hated anyone. I've got so I can't bear to think about him. I'd rather die than to ever let him touch me again. And I know if I go back around him, he'll either kill me or try to make me stay with him, like it was before."

"What do you plan to do?" Graben asked. "Not that it's any of my business."

"Lord, I don't know," she said, turning over on her back and looking at the sky. "I've been lying here wondering about it. I've never been anywhere away from home except when I was with Tobe Unger and that bunch, and I can't think of anywhere I can go that they won't find me. Right here on this mesa is the safest place I know of, but I couldn't stay here long without supplies."

Graben thought for a time. "I can leave you some of my grub, maybe enough to last a week. By then it might be safe for you to come down and go anywhere you want to go."

"I wish I could believe that," she said. "But if you think you can kill Tobe and all the others, you're out of your head. The Radners are with them now, and them Radners are like Indians. They are part Indian, but I don't know how much. You don't stand a chance."

"Can you handle a gun?" Graben asked after a moment.

"Not much. Mama and me could never afford shells for target practice. And Tobe wouldn't teach me because he was afraid I might use the gun on him. That's why Mama said I'd better leave the gun with her. She said I'd either miss you or get squeamish at the last minute and wouldn't be able to pull the trigger."

"So she got you to lure me up here close enough for her to get a shot at me?"

"Uh-huh," the girl said. "What did you have in mind when you asked if I could handle a gun?"

"It don't matter," Graben said wearily, pulling the blankets up to his chin. "A man would be a fool to give you a gun. Tobe Unger was right about that."

CHAPTER 7

The girl slept for a while. When she woke up, in the first gray light of dawn, Graben was saddling the buckskin. The wind had died down. It was still and cold on the mesa. The dark cedars stood motionless, as if waiting for the morning wind to animate them. The rocks waited for the sun to warm them. The rocks and the cedars would still be there long after the man and the girl were dust.

Graben wasn't sure about the dead-looking tangle of mesquite, which seemed to belong somewhere else.

"You leavin'?"

"That's right."

She noticed that the blue roan stood packed and ready to go. "I see you're takin' the roan."

"You can keep Picker's horse," he said, tightening the cinch.

"I won't keep him for long if Tobe Unger and them catch me ridin' him," she said.

Graben did not answer. That was her problem. He had his own to worry about.

The girl watched him throw on his saddlebags and blanket roll and lash them down behind the saddle.

"I can help you," she said. "I've been thinking about what you said last night. If you'll give me a gun, I won't try to use it on you. It's Tobe Unger and them I'm worried about. I know I won't ever have any peace as long as they're alive."

"Sorry," he said, not bothering to look at her.

She pushed herself up to a sitting position and stared at him with bitter eyes, her long pale hair in disarray. "That gun you took from Clyde Picker don't belong to you," she said in a trembling voice. "It's just as much mine as it is yours."

"I figger I've earned it," he said. "I figger I earned it the night they tried to kill me, and I figger I've earned it again tonight."

"You don't care what happens to me, do you?" she cried.

"I figger you'll get by all right," he said, picking up the lead rope. "Girls like you usually seem to manage, one way or another. And you could always go back to Tobe Unger, tell him you're sorry for everything, and wait for a chance to get your hands on a gun and put a bullet in him."

"And what do you think would happen to me if I did that?" she asked bitterly. "The others would kill me, but they'd have some fun with me first."

"Well, I hope they enjoy it," Graben said, stepping into the saddle. "But if I was them I don't know as I'd want to try it while I was wearing a gun. You might grab it and blow my head off."

"I just might," she agreed.

From the saddle Graben glanced at her. "I left some grub in that sack, but it won't last long if you go at it like you did last night. And if you intend to stay here long, you better drive that old plug back down off the mesa. He'll soon drink up all the water in that tank."

"You don't care about anyone or anything but yourself, do you?" she asked.

"It gets to be a habit after a while," he said. "I guess I've been around the wrong kind of people too much."

"Meaning me, I guess?"

"You're a smart girl," he told her. "That would have gone right by some people."

"Where are you goin'?" she asked.

"Where they won't have too much trouble finding me," he said. "In fact, they're liable to find me when they least expect it."

In spite of himself, Graben hated to leave her there like that. He even wanted to offer some word of sympathy, say he knew how she felt. After all, he himself had just lost a brother. But he could not bring himself to do it. He had trusted her when he should have known better and it had nearly cost him his life. Like a Judas goat, she had tried to lead him to the slaughter. She had betrayed him, and might do so again if given a chance.

With that thought in mind, he only nodded curtly and rode off on the buckskin, leading the blue roan, now reduced to a pack animal.

He could have left her a gun, he thought. But she was dangerous enough without one.

At the rim of the mesa Graben hesitated. The sun was still only a red promise in the east and he did not relish the thought of going down that steep trail with the blue roan right behind him. The roan, though sure-footed, was a high-spirited animal and preferred to set his own pace. If he became impatient with Graben's pace, he might try to crowd the buckskin. Annoyed at himself for not thinking of that when he was saddling up, Graben dismounted and shifted gear.

Then, mounting the roan, he started down the steep trail as the sun rimmed the horizon. The roan walked down the trail like a sensible horse and the buckskin docilely followed. At the bottom Graben let the roan find his own way through the rocks and brush and the rangy gelding had no trouble finding the way they had come in.

A short time later Graben was headed for a high rocky hill he had passed on his way back from Rock Crossing. He took up a position near the top of the hill and watched his back trail through field glasses bought with Frank's money.

Around noon he picked up seven riders, but they were not on his trail. They had either lost it or, more likely, decided there was no point in sticking to it. In any case, when Graben spotted them, they were headed toward Crazy Cora's shack.

He lowered the glasses. Seven riders. That meant the Radner boys were with them.

Graben raised the glasses for another look, but he was holding them where they were before and the group of riders had gone on beyond that point. He was about to shift the glasses when a lone rider appeared, a dark-garbed man on a dark horse who seemed to be following the Unger bunch.

"Picker!" Tobe Unger roared, tramping through the shack. "Where the hell is he? I told him to stay here till we got back!"

"His horse ain't in the corral, Tobe," Dub Astin said. "Just Crazy Cora's horse, lookin' mighty thirsty."

"Then water the damn horse! Then somebody get a fire goin'! Have I got to tell you bastards everything?"

He stepped to the shack door and saw the three Radner brothers riding off, as dark and silent as Indians. "Where the hell they goin'?"

It was Zeke Fossett, still in the saddle, who answered. "They said they were goin' on home to check on their horses and pick up some fresh ones. They said when we was ready we could come on over there and start from there."

"They did, huh? Why didn't they tell me that?" Without waiting for a reply, the big man scowled and barked, "Well, don't just sit there admirin' yourself. Didn't you just hear me say to get a fire goin' and cook some chuck? Barney, you can do that and Zeke and Dub take care of the horses."

"Why do I always end up doin' the cookin'?" Barney Kester asked.

"'Cause I say to, dammit!"

Later as they sat at the plank table wolfing down their grub, Dub Astin glanced through the window and said, "Rider comin', Tobe."

The attack on the beans and bread ceased as shaggy heads turned and hard eyes peered. Hands crept toward holstered guns.

Through the fly-specked window they could see the rider approaching at a walk—a tall slender man in black, riding a dark bay.

Barney Kester gulped and sputtered and pointed. "It's him!"

"Hell, it couldn't be," Dub Astin said. "We killed him. Didn't we, Zeke?"

"What the hell are you bastards talkin' about?" Tobe Unger growled.

"It's that man we saw at Turley's, the one who killed Chip!" Barney Kester gasped. "They said they killed him!"

"Wait a minute," Zeke Fossett said, peering through the window. A slow smile of relief spread across his sunburnt face. "That ain't him. I know who that is, but right now I can't recall his name. He rode with Mort Dudley and them for a while. I stopped at their ranch in New Mexico a few years back and that feller was there. Mort said he never knew anyone who could handle a gun like him. Later he was in the Barlow-Cushing war over around Hackamore."

"Sounds like a man we can use," Unger growled. "You sure it's him?"

"It's him all right. I'd know him anywhere."

"I can see now it ain't that feller we killed," Dub Astin said, as the silent stranger halted his dark horse before the shack.

"Then get on out there and tell him to come in," Tobe Unger said, with one of his rare startling smiles that made his big face seem even more ferocious. "Zeke, you keep a sharp eye on him as he comes through the door and give me a nod if it's the man you think it is."

"I still say it's the man we saw at Turley's," Barney Kester said. "I was half asleep but—"

"And blind drunk besides," Fossett snapped. "I tell you it's the man I saw in New Mexico."

"It won't hurt to be sure," Unger said.

A moment later Dub Astin came back in, followed by the dark silent stranger. Unger kicked back the chair at the end of the table and nodded for the tall lean man to sit down. The stranger did so, after a noticeable hesitation, his dark eyes circling the table in a brief glance.

"Get the man a plate and a cup, Dub," Unger said, as Astin was about to sit back down. Unger smiled at the stranger. "Zeke here tells me he's seen you before, but can't remember your name."

The stranger looked at the smiling Fossett and seemed to tense slightly. He did not say anything.

"Remember, I come by the Circle 8 in '79," Fossett said. "Mort Dudley told me you'd joined up with them not long before that. He said yore name, but I'm damned if I can remember what it was."

"Knell," the stranger said quietly. "Mark Knell."

"Yeah, that was it," Fossett said. "Now I remember. You and some of the others were playin' cards and you were winnin'. Chet Bowers said you always won. Whatever happened to old Chet anyway?"

"Dead," Knell said in the same quiet tone, as he accepted the plate of beans and cup of coffee Astin brought him.

"Dead?" Fossett said softly, his lopsided grin fading.

The stranger nodded. "There was some trouble around there. When I left they were all dead except Dudley and Snyder, and I heard they got it too."

"You mean they're all dead?" Fossett asked in disbelief.

"That's what I heard."

"What about you?" Unger asked. "You still game? If you are, I could use a man like you. We been havin' some trouble with a gun-fighter named Graben."

Mark Knell looked up with interest. "Frank Graben?"

"No, this one calls hisself Tom Graben. But some of the boys killed another man they think was his brother, so that one might of been Frank Graben."

Knell ate in silence, his face blank.

"Did you know Frank Graben?" Unger asked, watching him with

sharp, suspicious eyes.

Knell shook his head. "No, but I heard some talk about him a while back."

"What did you hear?" Unger asked.

"I heard he killed a bunch of men."

"It wouldn't surprise me," Unger said. "I never saw him myself, but from what the boys here said about him—he killed my kid brother. Now it looks like Tom Graben is out to get the rest of us. What about him? Did you ever hear of him?"

"I've heard the name Graben mentioned here and there, and sometimes I didn't catch the first name. So maybe it was Tom Graben they were talking about part of the time, instead of Frank."

"Well, whoever Tom Graben is, he's already caused us enough trouble," Unger said, darkly scowling. "More than enough. And I aim to get him before he kills the rest of us, one at a time. What do you say, Knell? I sure wouldn't mind havin' you around, if you ain't on your way to another job somewhere."

Knell shrugged. "Nothing that won't wait."

Seeing the dark rider had given Tom Graben a strange feeling. It had made him think of his dead brother. He had buried Frank with his own hands and knew it could not be him, yet the strange feeling remained.

Who could it have been? The stranger Gibby Tate had mentioned? And if so, why had he come back?

There were as yet no answers to the questions, and Graben did not waste much time thinking about it. With as little fuss as possible, he shifted his lookout to another rocky hill, one he had used before, in time to see the three Radners ride by on their way home.

There was the temptation to start shooting and whittle down the odds. But he held his fire and let them pass, unaware of how close they came. Though in his heart he knew better, he told himself that they might have thought it over and decided to stay out of it. But if he did not miss his guess they were only going home to check on their stock, the horses they had stolen from Belle Hopkins and other honest ranchers, and to pick up some fresh mounts before resuming the hunt for him.

Graben thought about Belle and the horses she had lost to thieves as he watched the Radners ride out of sight. It was common knowledge that they preyed on Belle's stock because she was a woman and they did not think she would do anything about it.

The one time when she had intended to do something about it, she and her hands had come upon Graben, nearly dead, before they got to Radner canyon and had turned back in order to save his life. He owed her for that, but if it could be avoided he did not want to take on the Radners until he had settled accounts with the Unger gang. The Unger gang came first.

And Graben liked to wait and see what men would do, even after he was fairly certain that he already knew. He wanted to wait and see what the Radners would do. If they came after him, they could take their chances. But he wanted them to make up their own minds.

Their minds were probably already made up, but he would wait until he was certain. After they were gone, he went down the rocky slope to his horses, mounted and rode to the ridge above Crazy Cora's shack.

He was just in time to see the stranger ride up to the shack and sit there on his dark horse until invited inside. Graben studied the man through his glasses and saw that he fitted the general description Gibby Tate had given of the man she had met on the trail.

After the men had watered his horse and gone inside, Graben studied the horse. From here it looked black, but it could have been brown or dark bay. Gibby Tate had said the stranger's horse was a dark bay and she probably knew what she was talking about, although most people seemed to have their own ideas about the color of horses. What one person said was a dark bay might look like a dark brown or even a black to someone else.

Graben remembered what had happened to him the night he had stopped at Crazy Cora's shack, and he wondered if the stranger was in the same danger now. He wanted to warn the man somehow, without getting himself shot again.

And he knew of only one sure way to do it.

Cupping his hands to his mouth, he shouted, "Better watch out down there, stranger! That bunch will offer you a meal and then shoot you in the back as you leave."

In the shack there was a tense moment. Only the stranger, Mark Knell, seemed relaxed and showed no surprise at Graben's shouted warning. He silently sipped his coffee and studied the faces of the other men at the table, his own face an unreadable mask.

Tobe Unger threw his big head up, startled, and his eyes flashed and glittered with excitement. Zeke Fossett's eyes widened with a look of fear and Dub Astin's mouth fell open. The little one, Barney Kester, spilled hot coffee down his chin and shirt front and, trembling with anger, jumped to his feet and ran bowlegged to the window, snaking out his gun. He broke the glass with his gun barrel and began firing at the rocks on the ridge.

Chairs scraped the plank floor as the others followed his example, Tobe Unger thrusting the indignant little man aside the better to study the ridge and watch for a target. Only Mark Knell remained seated at the table quietly drinking his coffee. But after a minute he too got up, slowly, and went outside, his gun still in the holster, and stood in the yard in plain view studying the rocks on the ridge.

Graben saw him standing there in the open, but could not decide what to make of it.

Then Tobe Unger came out with a gun in his hand and yelled, "See him?"

"No, but I see you," Graben grunted, bringing up his long-barreled Colt. He began firing and Unger dived back inside. But the stranger drew his gun and calmly returned Graben's fire, the lead whining off the rocks all around him. It was good shooting at that range, almost incredible shooting. Few men could have done as well with a rifle.

"Well, if that's how you want it," Graben said, a little sadly, and turned the long-barreled Colt on the stranger. His lead kicked up dust all around the man.

The stranger, his own gun empty, stood there calmly until Graben's gun was empty also, and then he walked unhurriedly back into the shack and closed the door. He had chosen sides, whether he knew it or not.

Chapter 8

Mark Knell silently reloaded his pistol, ignoring the excited glee of the others. If anything, his lean dark face seemed a little more solemn and gloomy than before.

"Them bullets was whinin' off them rocks all around him!" Dub Astin said. "I bet he was duckin' mighty fast!"

"I never saw anything like it," Tobe Unger agreed, watching Knell. "Where did you learn to shoot like that?"

"Here and there," Knell said. He holstered his gun and was silent a moment, frowning in thought. "If you boys wanted to see something, you should have seen his lead kicking up dust around my feet. He came closer to me than I did to him. And I've got a feeling he just missed me on purpose."

"Why would he do that?" Unger scoffed.

"That's what I'd like to know," Mark Knell said.

Graben reloaded the open-top Colt, got back into the saddle and rode back toward the mesa.

He could not help feeling betrayed by the stranger's show of ingratitude. It was not quite what he had expected after warning the man of the danger he might be in. He had hoped that if the stranger did not take his side against such men, he would at least remain neutral, and get away from the Unger bunch as soon as possible. But apparently he had decided to join up with them. Perhaps he preferred the company of thieves and murderers.

There was another reason why Graben felt let down. From a distance the stranger reminded him of Frank and he had hoped he might be the sort of man Frank was.

But what sort of man had Frank really been? And if he were still alive and if the Unger bunch had done nothing to antagonize him, would *he* have been so eager to take Tom's side? As boys they had nearly always been on opposite sides, and had seldom agreed about anything. It was something to think about, and it increased Tom Graben's mood of bleak disappointment as he rode on toward the mesa.

He suddenly halted, remembering that he had not intended to go back there. As he was trying to make up his mind, he saw Gibby Tate coming along the narrow trail through the rocks on the dead Clyde Picker's sorrel. She reined in, studying him uncertainly, a strange look coming into her pale green eyes—the look of a wild, hunted creature.

"I thought I heard shootin'," she said.

"Nothing serious. I was just welcoming the Unger bunch back. They're all over there, including your dark stranger."

"So he came back," she murmured as if to herself.

Graben nodded. "Looks like he's joined up with them, and he can outshoot all of them put together." A faint smile twisted his lips. "It's a good thing you didn't join up with me. The odds ain't getting any better. I saw the Radner boys headed for their place, but I figger they'll be back."

"You can't fight them all," Gibby Tate said, as if annoyed at his stubbornness and stupidity. "They'll kill you."

"They'll try," he agreed. "But some of them won't."

"You could kill half of them," she said, "and the others would still get you."

Graben shrugged. Discussing it was a waste of time. His decision had been made the night they had tried to kill him, and nothing had happened since to make him change his mind.

"What do you intend to do?" he asked. "If you're smart you'll get out of the country while Tobe Unger is busy with me, and never come back."

"What with?" she asked bitterly. "I ain't got a penny to my name, and no clothes fit to wear. Even this horse ain't mine."

Graben grinned. "I don't think Picker will complain about the horse."

"No, but somebody else might," she said. "The Radners sold him this horse, and they never had a horse they didn't steal."

"That's something to think about," Graben admitted, looking at the sorrel. The brand had been changed of course, but it was quite possible that the horse had once belonged to Belle Hopkins. It was a joke how well the Radner R would fit over the Hopkins H.

He glanced off toward the mesa she had just come from. "Did you drive that old crowbait back down like I told you?"

"No, he's still up there," she said. "I didn't even think about him. But if you're thinking what I think you are, I wouldn't start anywhere on him. I can't count on a stranger coming along every time I lose a horse in the middle of nowhere."

Graben shifted his eyes back to the sorrel. "You could ride that sorrel to the edge of the nearest town, and then take a stage or a train out of the country," he said.

"I might if I had the money for a ticket," she told him.

He met her glance. "If you really want to go, I'll give you the money."

She held out her hand, almost too quickly, he thought. "It's a deal!" she said.

He studied her silently for a time, and her bright green eyes did not waver. He noticed that in spite of the deep tan of her face, there were a few freckles across the bridge of her nose. The freckles reminded him of Belle Hopkins.

Slowly, he reached for Frank's wallet, counted out some money and handed it to her. "Here's a hundred dollars," he said. "There's a chance I won't live to spend it anyway. Buy yourself some clothes and use the rest on stage and train fare. Get as far away from here as you can. Get a job in a restaurant or a hotel till the right man comes along. Just make sure he is the right man this time."

She quickly stuffed the money in her pocket. Then she looked at him, and he did not like the look in her pale eyes. That look said as plainly as if she had spoken the words aloud, "If you think a hundred dollars will make up for killin' my mama, you're crazy." But she didn't say the words. She didn't say anything.

"What I told you is what I think you should do," he added. "But I can't make you do it. It's your life."

"That's right, it's my life," she said, and rode on by him without a word of goodbye.

He turned in his saddle to watch her and when she was fifty feet up the trail he called, "Hey, ain't you going the wrong way?"

"I'm going to watch the shack till they leave and then pick up a few of Mama's things," she said without stopping or looking back.

Graben opened his mouth to advise against it, but he knew she would not listen. So he shrugged and rode on to the foot of the mesa. He wanted to see Frank's grave again before they came after him. He might never have another chance.

Even before he dismounted he knew something was wrong. Some of the rocks had been pushed aside and the grave partly opened.

He thought he knew what had happened. Gibby Tate had discovered the grave and had dug down a piece thinking he might have buried money here.

Quietly seething with anger, he started to go after her. But he knew it would be a waste of time. She would either deny it or else she would have an explanation that would seem reasonable to her if not to him. And it would not surprise him if she had not fallen into Tobe Unger's clutches again by now.

Graben had no idea how right he was, for after leaving him Gibby Tate headed straight for the shack where she had grown up. Through the broken window they saw her coming down the rocky slope. Mark Knell saw her first, but said nothing. It was Astin who glanced through the window and said in surprise, "Here comes Gibby! Wonder what she's doin' here."

"That's what I'd like to know!" Tobe Unger cried angrily, tramping to the door and jerking it open. "What are you doin' here?" he roared as the girl rode down to the shack and dismounted. "Didn't I tell you to stay at Turley's?"

"I told you I wanted to see my mama," she answered breathlessly, coming meekly, almost fearfully toward him.

"Yore mama ain't here," Unger said. "She went off to Rock Crossin' after supplies. She should of been back by now. Something must of happened to her. Maybe she run into Tom Graben up in the hills and he shot her."

"You don't have to lie," the girl said, pushing in past him. "I already been here and talked to Clyde Picker. He told me everything."

"He did, huh?" Tobe Unger shouted. "Well, you just wait till I get my hands on him! Where the devil is he anyway?"

"He's dead. Tom Graben killed him."

She saw Mark Knell sitting in a chair with his back to the wall, but she did not say anything to him, and he remained silent, taking his cue from her.

"When did this happen?" Unger cried. "Has Graben been here?"

"Not as far as I know. That bastard Clyde Picker tried to attack me and I hit him with a skillet and got away. But he come after me again and Tom Graben killed him."

"I knowed that was Picker's horse," Dub Astin said.

"Where did it happen?" Unger asked.

"Over by that mesa. I found where Graben buried something and I wanted to see what it was. But just then Clyde Picker showed up and jumped me again, and Graben raised up out of the brush and shot him."

"What happened after that?" Unger asked suspiciously. "How did you get away?"

"It's a long story," she said with a weary sigh, smoothing back her pale hair. "And you wouldn't believe half of it even if I told you."

"You better tell me anyway," Unger said, watching her with hard bright eyes.

"Well, we spent most of the night on the mesa—"

"On the mesa?"

She nodded, watching the big man almost scornfully. "I got him up there so Mama could get a shot at him. If you think you killed her, forget it. She was still alive when I found her and I took her up on the mesa and doctored her wound. Then I got Tom Graben to go up there. We were gonna kill him and rob him, but Mama missed and he killed her. That's the only reason I came back. It wasn't you who killed her. It was Tom Graben."

Unger's face was a little pale. He took a deep breath. "What did she tell you?"

"She said she was gonna empty the shotgun at you for carryin' me off, but you shot her before she could get the hammers back. That's about what Clyde Picker told me."

Unger nodded. "That's how it happened. I had to shoot the old bitch or she would of filled me full of buckshot." Then he asked, "What happened after Graben shot her."

"I tried to get the gun and kill him myself, but he kicked it out of my hand," she said. "Then early this mornin' he rode off, and I didn't see him again until just now when I was on my way here. Then I met him on the trail and he told me I should get as far away from here as I could." She took the money out of her pocket and held it up. "He gave me a hundred dollars to buy clothes and a stage ticket with. But since I've decided not to leave, I can spend it anyway I want to."

"Give me that!" Unger cried, snatching the money out of her hand. "What did he give you this for, huh? What did you have to do to get it?"

"I didn't do anything!" she yelled. "He just gave it to me!"

"Don't hand me that!" Unger roared, striking her with his open hand and knocking her back against the wall. "You must of done something for it! What was it?"

"I already told you, I didn't do anything!"

"Like hell!" Unger bellowed. He slapped her again, then pushed her into a chair and pointed a finger in her face. "You stay there till I say you can move! I ain't done with you yet!"

He began counting the money and the weeping girl looked at Mark Knell in silent appeal for help. But he made no move to intervene, although he was frowning slightly—more at her, it seemed to Gibby, than at Unger.

Unger finished counting the money and glared at her. "A hundred dollars!"

"That's what I said it was!"

He leaned toward her and his big open palm again made her cheek burn and her ears ring. "A man don't give a girl that kind of money without she did something to earn it! How long were you with him anyway?"

"I already told you that too!" she screamed. "But I wish I'd stayed with him! Or left like he wanted me to! I was a fool to come back here! I never learn!"

"You sure don't!" Unger agreed. "But after I find Tom Graben and kill him, I aim to teach you! You're my woman and it's high time you started actin' like it!"

The girl looked up at him with hatred in her pale eyes, and then her eyes went to the double barrel shotgun on the pegs over the fireplace.

Following her glance, Tobe Unger said, "Don't worry, I'll be takin' Crazy Cora's scattergun with me. It wouldn't surprise me if Tom Graben don't get just what his brother got. Only this time I aim to make sure he's dead."

Tom Graben sat with his back against the mesa wall near the grave, chewing a piece of jerky. He had put the rocks back like they were, but he did not know how much good it would do, now that the grave had been discovered. It would have been better if he had not tried to disguise the grave at all, for then perhaps no one would have tried to open it in search of something that was not there. But he had not believed the grave would ever be discovered, and by rights it should not have been, camouflaged as it was. But evidently in searching the area for what he had lost, Gibby Tate had detected evidence that something had been buried there, and she had come back later to find out what it was.

He did not think she had dug down far enough to discover the body of his brother, but she might come back later, perhaps with help, to have another go at it. He had his doubts whether she would actually leave the country, as she had agreed to do. She might have never intended to leave, only promising to do so to get her hands on the money.

And perhaps he had never really believed she would go and had only given her the money because he had killed her mother, although the thought surprised him. If anyone had ever needed killing it was that bloodthirsty old woman, and the girl should have been punished for her part in Crazy Cora's scheme to murder him, not rewarded. But it was done now, and Graben didn't regret giving her the money. If he had ever owed her anything, the debt was paid now, and his conscience was clear. From now on she would have to get along without him. He wanted no one around him that he could not trust and rely on.

That was one reason he had spent so much time alone. In more than ten years of drifting he had met very few people whom he felt he could rely on completely, trust completely. Those he trusted usually disappointed him.

That was one thing about Frank. As boys they had seldom agreed about anything, yet he had never once doubted that Frank was telling the truth as he saw it. And if Frank had said he would do something, he would do it or break his back trying to do it. He would not let you down if he could help it. Tom Graben had not known very many people like that, and he could not help wondering if Frank had changed after he left home and found out what the world was like. Tom himself had not changed and he hoped Frank had not, but now he would probably never know for sure. The only one who could have told him was Frank himself, and Frank was dead.

One reason why he had remained here this long, when he should have been going, was that he wanted to see if the strange chill would come over him that he had felt before when near Frank's grave. But

in the daylight that feeling seemed far away and almost absurd, and
in fact, in all his years of wandering in far lonely places, Tom Graben
had never felt farther away from his brother than he felt at this moment, while sitting so close to Frank's grave. It was hard to believe
that Frank really was in the grave at all. Yet he knew Frank's body
was in the grave. At night he might almost have wondered, his imagination might have overpowered his reason, but in the daylight his
imagination slept, and the things you could not see at night were not
there in the daylight. In the daylight a man had only living enemies
to worry about, seen or unseen, and it was these that Tom Graben
had to think about now.

He reached for the open-top Colt, spun the cylinder and checked
the loads. Then he checked the Smith & Wesson pistols and got to
his feet, studying the two horses as he went toward them. In a fight
he might have to abandon the one carrying the pack, but for now he
decided to keep both animals with him, for he knew of no safe place to
leave either of them, nor any place where he could cache his supplies
with any certainty that they would not be found. Gibby Tate had destroyed his confidence in his ability to conceal anything.

As he stepped into the saddle he heard a shout and saw the Unger
bunch coming down the trail toward him, with Tobe Unger himself in
the lead and the dark-garbed stranger riding beside him.

Chapter 9

Graben started off at a gallop and did not look back until they began firing. Then he glanced over his shoulder and saw that they had spread out to avoid hitting one another.

Five riders. Five against one. But they had to catch him to kill him, and their horses were tired while his were rested.

Then he saw that one of them was leading the sorrel Gibby Tate had been riding. The horse was still saddled, but the girl was not in the saddle. They must have captured her and taken her horse to keep her from running off again. Or perhaps they had brought the horse along because it was fresher than their own. As fresh as or fresher than Graben's horses.

And as he began to draw away from them, he saw the man leading the sorrel swing onto the sorrel's back from his own mount without slackening his pace. Almost immediately that one began to draw ahead of the others. Graben thought it was the man named Fossett. Barney Kester, the logical choice for a fast ride because of his small size, was apparently not considered man enough to get the job done once he overtook Graben. It was an opinion Graben shared.

In any case, Graben had no intention of trying very hard to outrun just one man that he meant to kill anyway. But he would keep up the pretense of running until he and Fossett were far enough ahead of the others.

There was an old trail of sorts that led most of the way around the

foot of the mesa, and for the moment this seemed as good an escape
route as any—especially as much of the country bordering it was all
but impossible because of buttes and boulders and steep ridges and
deep ravines. Graben thundered past the cave and soon afterwards
the curving wall of the mesa hid the pursuing riders from his view.

On the shady side of the mesa he dipped into a shallow bowl floored
with rock and then curved around the pointed end of the mesa where
huge red boulders composed the wall and supported a few stunted
cedars in the crevices. Here the trail led off through more rocks, and
Graben rode behind one of these rocks and waited for Zeke Fossett.

Fossett, believing he had Graben stampeded, was riding hard
to overtake him. Bent low in the saddle, he galloped past the rock
where Graben waited, saw him out of the tail of his eye and turned
the sorrel so suddenly that the animal lost its footing and tumbled
screaming. Fossett scrambled from the saddle, hit the ground hard
and shoved up on one leg with a gun in his hand, fanning the hammer, all his shots going wild.

Graben leveled an identical gun at him, looked down the long
dark barrel and squeezed the trigger.

Fossett flopped to the ground a dead man.

Graben dismounted, shot the crippled sorrel and bent over the
dead man long enough to retrieve the shell belt and gun taken from
him months before. Returning to his horses he unbuckled Frank's
shell belt and holstered revolvers and shoved them into a saddlebag,
then buckled on his own belt and holster. He quickly reloaded the
open-top Colt, thrust it back into the holster and stepped into the
saddle. The Smith & Wessons were probably better guns but he was
used to the Colts. They felt right and natural in his hands, and he
knew what he could do with them.

In the saddle he hesitated briefly, looking back the way he had
come. Then he rode on through the rocks, heading for lower ground.

"Son of a bitch!" Tobe Unger roared a short time later, kicking the
dead man. "I should of knowed he couldn't take Graben by hisself!"

The other three were still in their saddles, looking soberly down
at the dead man—the dark-garbed silent Knell, the freckled toothy
Dub Astin, the bowlegged banty rooster Barney Kester.

"I knowed I should of come instead of him," Barney said.

Tobe Unger gaped at the little man in amazement, then laughed
harshly and shook his head as he walked back to his horse and got

back into the saddle.

They rode on, but at a much slower pace. The trail was difficult to follow over the rocky ground, and it was not long before Unger sent Barney Kester to get "them damn Indians," by which he meant the Radner boys, and some fresh horses!

So Barney Kester once more set off alone for Radner Canyon on an important mission, and he had not gone far when a quiet voice halted him in his tracks.

"You lost, Barney?"

Slowly, Barney Kester turned his head and saw Graben sitting the blue roan beside a big rock, the buckskin standing patiently to one side on a lead rope. It was, Barney realized, much the same fix Zeke Fossett had run into, and he did not want to end up like Zeke. So, although he began to tremble with rage and hatred and sheer frustration, Barney Kester was careful not to make any sudden movements with his hands.

He noticed that Graben had not drawn a gun this time, but for some reason that only made him more uneasy. It was almost as if the tall man was hoping he would draw.

Barney moved his hand a little farther away from his holstered gun and said, "You don't want to go causin' no trouble, Graben. A new man has showed up who can shoot as well as you or maybe even better. But I reckon you ought to know. I seen you duckin' up there on the ridge when his lead was flyin' all around you."

"Too bad he ain't here now, Barney," Graben said quietly. "If he was, he might save your life."

Barney Kester tensed. "I ain't scared of you, Graben."

"Is that why your teeth are chattering?" Graben asked. "Because you ain't scared?"

"My teeth ain't chatterin'."

"Sure they are. Listen."

Barney Kester listened for a moment, and sure enough, his teeth were chattering. He tried to stop the noise by clenching his teeth, and he stared at Graben's face with hatred. He saw how lean and hard that face was. It looked like it had been carved from solid rock and covered with leather. The eyes were like bits of frozen lake water with the sky's faded reflection trapped in the ice. Yet now and then Graben seemed to be smiling a little, but it was a mocking smile that fanned the flames of Barney Kester's hatred.

"Where you going, Barney?" Graben asked.

"That's my business," the little man said resentfully.

"You ain't going back to see the Radner boys again, are you, Barney?"

"What if I am?" Barney retorted. "There ain't nothin' you can do about it."

"Whatever gave you that idea? Just because it ain't any of my business, that don't mean there ain't anything I can do about it. I'm playing by your rules now, Barney. That means I can do anything I can get away with. So you better start being polite, even if you ain't had much practice at it."

Barney Kester trembled at these words. But much as he wanted to do, there was not much he could do, confronted as he was by a bigger, tougher, faster man. So he sat there and took it and even managed a sickly, painful smile. But within him his heart turned black with unbearable resentment. He hated everyone and everything, and silently cussed all those who had had any part in his creation—a botched job that never should have been attempted by incompetents. Yet here he was, an absurd little man who hated his absurdity and all those who reminded him of it. Tom Graben reminded him of it, just by being so tall and straight and ruggedly handsome and sure of himself, everything that Barney Kester was not.

Barney thought of ways he might survive a fight with Graben. He could throw himself off his horse and use the animal for cover while he fired at Graben. Or he could pull some trick like starting to unbuckle his gun belt, then suddenly going for his gun.

But so many things could go wrong. And he was not at all sure that he could make his move quick enough. There were men who could draw a gun and fire it—and hit what they were shooting at —before you could blink an eye. Barney Kester did not know how it could be done, yet he had seen it happen, or caught the indistinct blur of movement and seen the results of it. And all those things people said could not be done with a handgun—they had been done repeatedly despite what all the scoffers said. At a carnival in St. Louis Barney had once seen a trick shooter put six slugs in a playing card nailed to a tree twenty feet away in a few split seconds—by fanning the hammer of the gun, something almost everyone said could not be done. Zeke Fossett had fancied himself a gun fanner and that was probably what had got him killed, for he had not been any good at it. But some men were. Gunfighters usually did not show off like that trick shooter, but some of them could probably do what he had done, and it would not surprise Barney Kester in the least if Graben could do it.

No, the smart thing for Barney Kester to do was to talk his way out of this somehow and never tell Unger and the others about seeing Graben here. Then he could watch for his chance to kill Graben, or help do it, with little or no risk to himself.

"What are you waiting for, Barney?" Graben asked. "Are you waiting for me to turn my back and start riding off? Or are you waiting for your friends to show up and give you a hand?"

Barney Kester's eyes got red with bloodlust, and his face twitched and quivered with the burning desire to jerk out his gun and fill the tall man full of lead. But other men who had tried that were roasting in hell, and Barney Kester had no wish to join them.

"It ain't like I'm picking on a runt, Barney," Graben added, rubbing salt in the wound. "Sam Colt made all men equal. So you can't hold your size against me."

Barney Kester gritted his teeth and said, "I ain't gonna draw on you, Graben. I ain't about to give you no excuse to kill me."

Graben stared at him in open amazement. "Ain't you forgetting something, Barney? Ain't you forgetting the night you bastards tried to kill me?"

"That wasn't me," Barney mumbled. "That was Tobe and the others."

"It was you and Unger and Fossett and Astin," Graben said. "You were the ones who followed me out. The others were crowded behind you four at the door, so maybe they didn't get a shot at me. But I know you were standing outside near Unger, watching me as I started to get in the saddle, and the moment my head was turned you four started shooting."

"Ain't you forgettin' Mac Radner?" Barney asked. "He ain't that much taller than me. That was him you saw and in the dark you just thought it was me."

"Mac Radner stayed in the house," Graben said. "He's the only one who didn't get up when I started to leave. That's why I was hoping him and his brothers would stay out of it. I've got no quarrel with them, so far. But if Unger keeps sending you over there after them, they're sure to get in it and then I won't have any choice in the matter."

"They're already in it," Barney Kester told him. "They only went home to check on their stock and pick up some fresh horses. I figger they're already on their way back over there by now. They prob'ly heard that shootin' and cut over this way to get in on it. They prob'ly ain't far from here right now. If you shoot me, they'll be on you like a hawk on a chicken."

Graben smiled the coldest smile Barney Kester had ever seen. It froze Barney's heart with icy dread. "The Radners can't save you now, Barney," he said. "No one can. No one except me. I can't decide whether to kill you now or let you live a little while longer. I've looked forward to it now for quite a while and I don't want it over with too soon. It's going to be awful dull around here after you boys are all dead. There won't be much a man like me can do around here."

Barney Kester did not trust himself to speak. He knew that Graben was just playing with him, and the thought was almost unbearable, but perhaps it was better than the alternative.

"Tell you what," Graben said. "I'm going to leave it up to you, Barney. You can ride back and tell Unger you couldn't find the Radner boys and I'll let you live a while longer. Or you can go the other way and I'll kill you now. The choice is yours. It don't really matter to me one way or the other."

"He'll know I lied," Barney said.

Graben shrugged with complete indifference. "I never said he'd believe you. But I doubt if he'll kill you for it. He's getting a little short-handed. I reckon that's why he sent you after the Radner boys."

"That ain't the reason," Barney said. "They can foller a trail better than us."

"You can tell Unger he won't need no trackers to find me, Barney," Graben said. "I'll find him when I'm ready."

Barney Kester sat tense and silent in his saddle, afraid to look at Graben, afraid Graben would see the terrible struggle going on inside him. His teeth were clenched and his red face glistened with sweat.

"You don't have to decide now, Barney," Graben told him. "I'll give you about another thirty seconds to think about it."

Barney Kester wrenched himself out of the grip of his private demon, and without saying a word or looking at Tom Graben he turned his horse and rode back the way he had come.

Graben looked after the little man with a faint smile on his lips, and when Kester was out of sight he turned into a nearby gully and followed it down through the rocks until he came to the main trail to Radner Canyon. He halted beside the trail and waited.

Before long he saw the three Radners coming unhurriedly up the steep trail, their dark eyes on the ground. They were wearing their threadbare store suits and uncreased black hats, and their well-oiled guns.

They did not see Graben until he rode into the trail above them and sat the blue roan facing them, holding the lead rope in his reins hand. But he had not drawn a gun and he seemed relaxed in the saddle. He was almost smiling and there was a friendly look on his hard weathered face as they halted their horses in surprise and looked up at him.

"You boys looking for me?" he asked quietly.

They stared at him in silence for about a minute, their dark eyes and brown faces impassive. Then Mac Radner's dark eyes glinted a little. But he slowly shook his head and said, "We're lookin' for some strayed horses. Don't guess you've seen 'em?"

Graben shook his head. "I don't think you will either, not around here." He folded his hands on the horn and leaned forward in the saddle, nodding past them down the trail. "I doubt if they ever left the canyon. You should take a better look down there before you go hunting for them anywhere else. Besides," he added with a cold smile, "somebody might get the wrong idea about what you're looking for."

The deadly glint returned to Mac Radner's black eyes. "We'll just take a look up there a piece," he said.

Graben did not move aside to let them pass. His face became bleak and old. "Sorry, boys," he said. "This trail's closed. It would be too risky to go any farther."

It was the youngest Radner, a boy with a mean stubborn face, who made the mistake of going for his gun, and Graben shot him out of the saddle.

"Too bad," he said, training the long-barreled Colt on the other two. "I was sort of hoping you boys would stay out of it. Now I don't guess there's much chance of that."

They looked down at their dead brother lying at the edge of the trail, and then their hard silent eyes returned to Graben.

"But I don't guess it really matters," he added as if to himself. "Sooner or later I'd have to come after you anyway. You boys have got a bad habit of stealing horses from the wrong people. One of them did me a good turn a while back, and I wouldn't want to be worried about what might happen if they took a notion to come after their horses themselves."

Neither Mac nor Hump Radner said anything. They continued

to watch him in a silence that throbbed with hate. Their smoldering black eyes longed to murder him on the spot, but his smoking gun warned them to wait for a better time.

He gestured with the gun. "Take your brother back and bury him. Then do whatever you're a mind to. If you decide to come after me, I won't be hard to find."

He watched in silence while they got down and lifted their dead brother across his saddle and rode back down the trail without looking back. Then he turned his horses around and rode slowly back toward the mesa.

He had not gone far when he met Barney Kester coming along the trail.

CHAPTER 10

After leaving Graben, Barney Kester had got to thinking, always a dangerous thing for a man like Barney, whose mind was obsessed with the need to get even with the world and in the process prove that, in his own way, he was just as big a man as anyone, and a lot smarter than most.

Anyway, after thinking about it, Barney could see no good reason why he should do as Graben had told him to do. On the other hand, there was a very good reason why he should do what Tobe Unger had told him to do. If he didn't, Tobe would make him regret it.

And Barney wanted to do it to spite Graben and prove that he could do it. Barney wanted to show them all, but especially Graben.

He figured that Graben would avoid the main trail to Radner Canyon and Barney selected this as his route. He could make better time on the trail, and also he had a hunch he would meet the Radner brothers coming back along it. Then he would lead them back to Unger and the others, proving that once again he had been able to get past the enemy and carry out his mission when perhaps no one else could have done so.

Having made his decision, Barney cut through the rough country and turned along the trail at a lope. When he heard the shot it startled him for a moment. But then he told himself that one of the Radners had probably shot something for dinner, and he urged his horse to an even faster pace, hoping to overtake the man before he got home with his kill. The farthest thing from Barney's mind was that he might run into Graben on the trail.

When he rounded the curve in the trail and saw Graben approaching at an east trot, leading the packed buckskin, his eyes popped out in alarmed disbelief. He saw the look of surprise on Graben's hard face, followed by the red flush of anger, and this time Barney knew he would not be able to talk his way out of it.

Almost without thinking, Barney swerved his horse off the trail and pounded away through the brush and rocks.

A shout rose in Graben's throat but died there. He knew Barney Kester would not heed any command to stop. It would be a waste of breath. So Graben also left the trail and made himself a path through the gray brush and red rocks.

But he was encumbered by the led horse and the next time he saw Barney Kester the little man was bent low over the neck of his horse, racing away over the hill like a scared rabbit.

Graben thought about abandoning the buckskin temporarily, decided against it, and tore his way through the brush to more open ground. Then he galloped up the slope to the crest of the hill and saw Kester streaking over the next ridge. If the little man was not leaving the country he was certainly giving a good impression of it.

Graben had halted for a moment before he caught sight of Kester outlined briefly on the far ridge. He was about to resume the chase when Belle Hopkins rode out of some nearby rocks and asked, "Why are you chasing that little guy?"

Graben met her questioning blue eyes and frowned. "That little guy," he said, "happens to be Barney Kester, one of Tobe Unger's more poisonous snakes."

"Still," she said, "it doesn't seem quite right for a big strong man like you—"

"Swallow it!" Graben snarled. "He was big enough to shoot me in the back, and I was thinking strongly about doing the same to him when I got close enough. Then you had to come along. What are you doing here anyway?"

"Looking for you," she told him. "I figured you'd be in need of a nurse again by now."

"No thanks," he told her.

She studied his face in silence for a moment, and then asked, "What are you so angry about?"

He stared at her with cold eyes. "I appreciate all you've done for me," he said. "But this is something I've got to do my way, and I've got to do it alone. It's going to be hard enough to do what I've got to do without worrying about you."

"And what happens if you get shot up again?" she asked. "Who's going to take care of you?"

"The buzzards," he told her. "They'll finish the job next time. I figgered you had sense enough to know that."

She watched him for a moment with no expression on her freckled face or in her clear blue eyes. Then her face reddened with anger. "A lot of good it did to haul you out of these hills and nurse you back to health," she said. "As soon as you're well enough you come right back here to give them another chance at you."

Graben found it hard to meet her accusing glance. "Maybe it don't make much sense," he admitted. "But it's something I've got to do and talking about it won't change anything. It will just make it harder for both of us."

She again studied him in that silent, clear-eyed way she had. Then she sighed and shook her head. "I had a feeling I was wasting my time," she said. "Why I ever bothered with you in the first place I'll never know."

"I've wondered about that some myself," Graben replied. "But like you said, you'd do the same for anyone. Even one of Unger's men, I guess."

She thought for a moment, and then said as if surprised, "I guess I would."

He grinned. "Well, maybe you better bring a wagon the next time you come back this way. Some of them may need doctoring, if any of them are still alive."

"You plan to kill them all?" she asked.

"I plan to try," he told her.

"Just for trying to kill you?"

"It's a little more than that now," he said. "But I'd just as soon not go into it."

"What is it with you?" Belle Hopkins asked. "Why do you have to keep everything to yourself?"

He sighed wearily, glancing off in the direction Barney Kester had gone. No chance now of overtaking the little man. Quite possibly Belle Hopkins had saved Barney's life, but he saw no point in mentioning it. "I've found it's usually best to keep my mouth shut," he said. "No one's ever agreed with very much I had to say, or liked me any better for saying it. And some things sort of belong to a man, things he can't share with anyone else. Most of my life's been like that. What means something to me wouldn't mean the same to anyone else."

"I know what you mean," she said. "I've felt that way about a lot of things myself."

He nodded. "It sort of changes some things to talk about them, though some people don't seem to feel that way. They seem to think that's the only purpose anything has, just having something else to talk about."

"Well, no one can ever accuse you of that," Belle Hopkins assured him.

"I don't know," he said with an uneasy grin. "Lately I've been running off at the mouth pretty bad. I've already passed up two chances to kill that little fellow you saw, just so I'd have somebody to talk to the next time he came along."

"Really?" she said in surprise. "There may be hope for you yet. You may turn out to be human after all."

"I wouldn't expect any miracles overnight," he said dryly. "Now you best be heading back. Everybody around Rock Crossing will be out looking for you." He gave her a sharper glance. "That wasn't what you had in mind, was it? You come traipsing over this way by yourself, knowing all along that these hills would soon be swarming with searchers who might decided to take a hand in this whether I like it or not—is that your game?"

She looked at him with still eyes. "Just when I was beginning to think there might be a little hope for you. No, that isn't my game. I knew you'd never forgive me if I spoiled your fun. So I decided to let you go ahead and get yourself killed if that's what you want. I only rode over this way to see if it had already happened. I didn't want to spend the rest of my life wondering what happened to you—and I had a feeling you wouldn't come back even if you could. You'd ride on when it was over and I'd never know if you were alive or dead."

"I meant to send you a letter," he said.

She looked at him carefully. "Then you weren't planning to come back?"

Graben heaved a sigh. "I don't think it would be a good idea."

"Why not?' she asked.

"I don't belong there," he said.

"Where do you belong?"

He glanced about at the lonesome cedar-dotted hills. "Here," he said, as if surprised. "Or some place like this."

"There aren't many places like this left," Belle Hopkins told him. "The country's filling up. Before long there'll be settlers moving into the few that are left. You might as well join the crowd. Sooner or later you'll have to."

"I intend to put if off as long as I can," he said. "There are still a few places left where a man can be alone and breathe air that somebody else ain't breathed for a spell."

"Is that what you didn't like about being at the ranch?" she asked. "It was too crowded for you?"

"That was part of it. I get edgy if I have to be around people very much. But that wasn't the main reason."

She studied his face, but he avoided her glance. "Did it have anything to do with me?" she asked.

He sighed and shifted uncomfortably in his saddle. "I'm a saddle tramp," he said. "That's all I've been since I left home and I guess that's all I'll ever be. I hate being tied down in one place or being in any kind of situation where I can't leave anytime I take a notion without having to explain to anyone. A man like that don't ever amount to anything."

Belle Hopkins was silent and thoughtful for a time, not looking at him. Then she's said, "You're always welcome to come back there anytime you take a notion, and you can leave again anytime you like. You won't even have to tell me goodbye if you don't want to. I'll understand."

Then she turned her horse and rode off without another word, and Graben, looking after her, did not know anything to say.

He turned his own horse and rode back the way he had come, Barney Kester momentarily forgotten. But there was a sudden feeling of discontent in him and a desire to get this over with as quickly as possible, and that brought Kester back into his thoughts.

He did not think Kester would keep going the way he was headed. He would probably do one of two things. He would either circle around and head for Radner Canyon, or he would circle in the other direction and head back to find Unger and the others. And if the little man was as stubborn and spiteful as he seemed, it would probably be the former. He would want to show everyone, especially Graben, that he could do what he had set out to do.

Graben suddenly halted and considered for a moment. He had

ridden along the canyon rim some days back, and there were only a few places where a man on horseback could descend. He knew of only one such spot on this side of the main trail. Barney Kester was probably on his way there now, but Graben, being closer, might get there before he did.

Turning his horse, Graben rode along the slope between the crest of the ridge where he might be seen and the thick brush in the narrow valley where the going would be too difficult. But when the worst of the brush was behind him, he angled across the valley and hid his horses in the rocks near the break in the canyon rim. Then he waited, blending in with the gray brush and the rocks.

He checked the open-top Colts and slid them back where they belonged, but kept his right hand near the one in his waistband.

On the way down here he had thought about what he had in mind and had concluded that it was the thing to do. Barney Kester would try to avoid a fair fight that he might lose, but given the chance he would not hesitate to shoot Graben from behind or from ambush, and he was the type to dance on a dying man and gloat over the corpse.

Before long Graben saw the little man slipping along on his horse through the rocks and stunted cedars. When Barney saw the gap in the rim opening before him, an exultant smile lit up his badly shaped little face. He turned his head and cast a quick glance up toward the rocky eroded hills and he stuck out his tongue as if he thought Graben might be up there somewhere watching him, perhaps with field glasses. His tongue was still partly exposed when he looked ahead again and saw Graben standing there at the edge of the gap through which he had hoped to pass. He stared in disbelief at that hard, hated face and saw the cold shine of contempt in Graben's blue eyes.

"Sorry, Barney," Graben said. "I got no more time for games."

But even this time Graben was not prepared for the swiftness of the little man's reaction. Barney left his saddle and dived aside into the rocks as if diving into a river. Graben could hear him scrambling away through the boulders. Cussing softly, Graben himself drew a gun and darted for cover.

Then he heard a shrill laugh and Kester's taunting voice. "What good is yore size and speed with a gun now, Graben? You got to come after me, and you never saw the day you could sneak up on Barney Kester! I'll be waitin' to plug you!"

"I didn't think you wanted to fight!" Graben retorted.

"I didn't! But you didn't give me no choice, did you?"

"Sure I did! I told you you could fight or ride back the way you came! But you started playing games!"

"You ain't my boss, Graben! I do what Tobe Unger tells me, not what you tell me!"

"Doing what he tells you will get you killed, Barney! If you'd done like I told you it might have saved your life!"

"Come and get me, Graben!" the little man jeered. "I figger I'm as good at this game as you are! Maybe better!"

"All right, Barney, if that's how you want it," Graben muttered to himself, and began working his way through the rocks along the canyon rim. He passed near his horses, but left them where they were and continued on foot, now circling away from the rim to come up behind Kester. Twice he heard the little man call his name, the first time sounding a little worried, the second in a shrill frightened tone. But Graben did not answer, not wanting to give his position away.

And finally he came out of the brush behind Barney and saw him crouched behind the rock. Barney was facing the other way, now and then peering over the rock in the direction he thought Graben to be.

After a while something made him glance around and he saw Graben standing there, no more than fifteen feet away. But this time Barney's reaction was not so swift. For a moment he remained crouched there, like some stupid bug which, even after its rock had been removed, still believed itself hidden.

He had a gun in his hand, but he did not try to bring it around to bear on Graben, for he knew he would never be able to get his shot off in time. All Graben had to do was squeeze the trigger.

"Sorry, Barney," Graben said, but without much pity for a man who deserved none. "I can't let you off this time. It's time to settle your account."

Just as he was about to squeeze the trigger, Graben heard a shout and saw a rider walking his horse through the rocks and cedars about two hundred yards away. Unger's men had scattered out to search for him and were calling back and forth to one another.

Barney Kester's lips began to twitch and his small crooked teeth were bared in a smile. "You don't dare shoot me, Graben," he said. "If you do, they'll be on you like a hawk on a chicken. You'll be trapped between them and the canyon. And if you try goin' down in the canyon, you'll have the Radners to worry about."

Graben could see that for himself. "You've got the devil's luck," he muttered. "It looks like you may last a while yet, unless you force me to kill you."

Barney shrugged. "I ain't no fool," he said.

"Don't move," Graben said. He went toward the little man and took the gun from his hand. "Now get down on your belly and stay there." As Barney started to obey him, Graben brought the gun down on his head and Barney went limp without a sound.

Then Graben turned his attention to the riders working their way around the foot of the hill. He caught only fleeting glimpses of them through the rocks and cedars. They were not all abreast, but in a ragged line with one man well ahead of the others. It was the dark-garbed stranger, and Graben, watching tensely, saw him pause near his trail. The man must have seen his tracks, and Graben waited for him to sound the alarm. But after a moment, to his surprise, the man rode on in the same direction and at the same slow pace he had been going.

Graben could not hope for the same consideration from the others, and he did not want to be here when they crossed his trail. Going to his horses, he led them through the rocks along the rim, going in the opposite direction to that of the Unger men.

When he believed he was safely behind them, he stepped into the saddle and headed back up into the hills at a walk, keeping out of sight in the rocks and stunted cedars as much as possible.

Just when he was beginning to think he was in the clear he heard Barney Kester yelling in a shrill voice, "Look out, Tobe! He's gettin' away!"

Chapter 11

Cussing himself for not hitting Kester harder, and tying him up and gagging him while he was at it, Graben heeled the blue roan into a trot and pulled the buckskin after him. To go any faster would have made too much noise and perhaps brought the hunters after him that much quicker. If possible he wanted them to waste some time trailing him to this point, thus giving him that much more time to get away.

If it had only been Tobe Unger and Dub Astin back there, he would not have tried to get away from them. But he had no wish to fight the dark-garbed stranger, and he had a feeling that the stranger was a lot more dangerous, when he wished to be, than the other two combined, and Barney Kester thrown in.

He could still hear Barney yelling his lungs out, telling them which way he figured Graben had gone, and someone else—it sounded like Astin—recommending that they all ride straight for Kester and pick up the trail at that point, rather than waste any more time. Their voices were growing fainter by then, for Graben was already well up into the barren rocky hills.

That was what they did. Tobe Unger, Dub Astin and Mark Knell converged on Barney Kester, who had been ordered to stay where he was and show them the trail. When they arrived, the little man was standing by his horse, peering down at some faint tracks on the hard rocky ground. He avoided their eyes, especially the hard glittering eyes of Tobe Unger.

The big man scowled murderously at him. "Where's yore gun?"

"He took it!" Barney cried. "The bastard got the drop on me from behind and—"

"I don't want to hear that again!" Unger barked, his face turning purple with rage. "About how he got the drop on somebody else from behind! You never should of let him sneak up on you! And what was you doin' way off down here anyway, instead of goin' after the Radners like I told you?"

Barney thought quickly. He could not bring himself to admit that he had gone so far out of his way to avoid Graben. No, that would never do. So he said instead, "I saw Graben headin' down this way and I come after him. But the bastard was layin' for me and—"

"You never should of tried to take him by yoreself," Unger growled. "But it's done now and we've already wasted too much time. You go on and get the Radners like I told you to begin with, and the rest of us will get on his trail."

When Kester was gone, Dub Astin scratched his stubbled chin and said, "I got a idea that might save us a little time."

"What?" Unger grunted.

"It's gonna take us a while to find any tracks on this hard ground that we can foller," Astin said. "Why don't one of us ride on ahead and try to cut his trail, then fire a shot to bring the others?"

"I could do that," Mark Knell said quickly.

Unger hesitated, then reluctantly nodded. "All right, go ahead."

Dub Astin opened his mouth as if to speak, but remained silent until Knell had ridden off. Then he said, "I doubt if he'll try too hard to find that trail."

Unger gave him a sharp glance. "What do you mean?"

Astin hooked a thumb over his shoulder. "I saw him stopped up there earlier, lookin' at the ground. Then he rode on. But I got curious and drifted down that way. I got there about the time Barney started yellin', so I come on back down this way and never said nothin'. But what Knell was lookin' at on the ground was the tracks of Graben's horse headin' this way, only he rode on past there and never said nothin'. That's why I don't reckon he'll try too hard to find Graben's trail this time."

"Why didn't you tell me?" Unger asked angrily.

"I started to. Then I figgered it might be better to stay quiet and keep a eye on him till I got a chance to talk to you in private. What

I'm wonderin' now is, why was he in such a hurry to go on ahead to cut Graben's trail hisself, when he already cut it once and never said nothin' to nobody about it."

Tobe Unger scowled off in the direction Knell had gone, his thick dark brows knitting in anger.

"What you figger he's up to?" Astin asked.

"I don't know," Unger said. "But I've had a feelin' all along there was something wrong about him. It was too good to be true, a man like him showin' up just when we needed someone like him. Our luck ain't been goin' that well lately."

"I ain't been so shore any of the time it was such a blessin', him showin' up," Astin said, squinting his bloodshot eyes into the hot afternoon sunlight. "I kept thinkin' about what he said about all them boys he rode with in New Mexico bein' dead. If we ain't real careful, we're liable to end up the same way if we count on him at the wrong time. He's liable to turn on us just when we need him the most."

"We'll keep a eye on him and try to find out what he's up to," Unger said. "But for now don't say nothin' about what you told me."

"That's how I figgered you'd want to do it," Astin said, with a grin. "That's why I never said nothin' before."

It took them two hours to follow the tracks to the main trail that led to Radner Canyon, and there in the trail they found Mark Knell waiting for them.

"I crossed the trail farther up," Knell said, nodding in that direction. "There were so many tracks I couldn't tell whether any of them were his or not, so I kept going. But I didn't find anything farther on so I doubled back. Even now I'm not positive he went up the trail, but he must have."

It sounded like too much explaining for a man who normally had so little to say, and Unger and Astin exchanged a narrow glance.

Then Unger scowled at the man in black and said, "Maybe you ain't as good at readin' sign as you are at handlin' a gun."

"I never said I was," Knell replied quietly, glancing at the shotgun balanced across the saddle in front of Unger.

Just then Dub Astin said, "Here comes old Barney, and he's by hisself." Astin was always peering about through his narrow bloodshot eyes, hoping to be the first to spot anything of interest and report on it. The easygoing Texan was a more dangerous man than he appeared to be.

Unger and Knell looked in that direction and saw Kester coming up the trail. Even before he reined to a halt, Unger barked, "Where's the Radners?"

"They wouldn't come," Barney said uneasily, wiping his sweaty palm on his trousers.

"What do you mean they wouldn't come?" Tobe thundered at him.

"Graben has killed Ed Radner," Barney said, "and Mac and Hump was buryin' him. I couldn't even hardly get their attention. They wasn't cryin' or nothin', they just looked mad as hell and never said nothin'."

"Why didn't you bring back some fresh horses?" Unger asked, hoarse with anger and frustration. It wasn't enough that he had a gunfighter against him. He could not rely on his own men to do anything right. At times even they seemed to be working against him, either through treachery or stupidity.

"I never even thought about it," Barney admitted worriedly. "But I doubt if them two would of even answered me if I had asked them to loan us some horses. They prob'ly blame us partly for Ed bein' dead. But I guess they mostly blame Graben."

"They never said what they aim to do about it?"

"They never said nothin'. Barely grunted when I asked if it was Graben killed him. But from the look in their eyes I don't think I'd want to be in his place. Them two breeds looked like they was about ready to go on the warpath."

"I guess they'll try goin' after him by theirselves," Unger said resentfully. "But we can't count on them havin' any more luck than we've had. The only way we can be sure he's dead is to get him ourselves." He swung his horse up the trail. "Let's go! We've wasted too much time already."

The others fell in behind him and as they rode they watched both sides of the trail for any sign of tracks leaving it, but saw none. They passed the bulk of the mesa off to their left, looking like a huge ship surrounded by smaller boats on a stormy sea, and continued on along the narrow winding trail through the rocks.

They were now less than a mile from Crazy Cora's shack, and Tobe Unger had been thinking about the wild beautiful girl he had left there, and about the time she had spent with Tom Graben.

"Where's he think he goin'?" Unger cried hoarsely.

Just then, as his horse brushed the limbs of a cedar that grew out over the trail, a gun exploded in the rocks off to the right and the bullet nicked his hat brim.

All four men leapt from their saddles, scrambled for cover among the rocks and began firing at the white puff of smoke they had seen. But no more shots were fired back at them and they saw no sign of anyone in the rocks. Their own guns fell silent and they waited, puzzled.

"Think we got him?" Dub Astin asked.

No one bothered to answer. The others kept peering in the direction from which that one shot had come.

"It's some kind of trick," Barney Kester said, his small face twisted with bitterness and hatred. "I bet he ain't even up there. He prob'ly just fired that one shot to keep us here till dark, while he sneaks off and gets away!"

Tobe Unger turned his glittering eyes on the little man. "Why don't you go take a look, Barney. See if he's still up there."

Barney swallowed, and then his face got red with resentment. "Why do you always pick me to do all the dirty and risky work?"

"Because you're always runnin' yore big mouth when you should keep it shut," Unger said savagely. "Now get on up there and see if he's still there or not."

Barney Kester began to tremble with fear and hatred. Even after all the close shaves he had had lately, he was still more afraid of Tobe Unger than he was of Graben. But right now he also hated him more, and his fear and hatred were at war inside him.

"Hell, you might of got him with that scattergun, Tobe," Dub Astin said. "If he had his head up you prob'ly did, even if you never saw him when you shot."

"You hear that, Barney?" the big man growled. "You ain't got a thing to worry about."

"I ain't got a gun," Barney said weakly. "He took mine, remember?"

"Take mine," Unger said, flicking the big Remington from his holster as if it did not weigh an ounce. But when he handed the gun to Barney its weight sagged in his little hand. Unger nodded toward the rocks. "Now hurry it up. He's either dead or gone. If he was still up there we would of heard something else out of him by now."

There probably was no real danger, Barney decided. And he could look like a hero without running any real risk, for he felt certain Graben was not up there in those rocks.

Unger and Astin were watching him, the former with an impatient scowl, the latter with an encouraging grin. The silent stranger,

Knell, kept his somber dark eyes on the rocks.

"Well, here goes," Barney said, and began wriggling away through the rocks. He was soon out of sight, and the other three waited in silence, occasionally mopping sweat from their drawn faces. The day was almost gone, but the rocks had baked in the sun all day and absorbed a lot of heat. The cold night wind would drive it away just when it was needed.

After a time, Kester suddenly stood up in the rocks, waving one hand over his head and holding a gun in that hand. "It's all right!" he called. "It was a trick, like I figgered! He wasn't here none of the time." The little man came back down through the rocks, still holding the gun. "He just tied a string to that cedar and to the trigger of the gun and it went off when yore horse brushed against the tree."

"Let me see that!" Unger said, taking the gun from Kester's hand. He looked at the gun and then glared at Barney. "Yore gun!"

Barney sadly nodded, and exchanged the big Remington for his smaller piece.

"He never would of left one of his own guns here," Unger said. "But he didn't mind leavin' yores. It didn't cost him nothin'."

"It nearly cost him his life," Barney said, but no one appeared to believe him.

Unger scowled darkly at him for a moment, then glanced at the sun sinking in the west and splashing the rocks around them with its dying crimson light. "Well, he's got away again," the big man said bitterly. "We can't track him in the dark, and no tellin' where he'll be by mornin'."

He got back in his saddle and the others returned to theirs. The horses, trained to stop the moment the rider's weight left the saddle, and exhausted besides, had stopped almost in their tracks. Knell's dark bay was considerably fresher than the other animals, and after glancing about for a moment he said, "It might save a little time in the morning if we knew which way he went. If you don't mind I think I'll fool around here for a while."

Unger and Astin exchanged a silent glance, the Unger grunted, "Suit yoreself," and he rode on to Crazy Cora's shack with Astin and Kester at his heels. He noticed with some relief that Crazy Cora's lame horse was still in the corral. If Gibby was gone she had left on foot and would not have gone far.

Leaving his horse for the others to take care of, he strode into the shack and saw her sitting at the plank table. She looked up at him with hatred in her pale eyes.

"Looks like you're still here," he grunted.

"I ain't goin' nowhere till I get my money back," she told him.

He sneered. "How you aim to do that?"

She glanced at the shotgun in his big hands. "I'll find a way."

Scowling, he unloaded the shotgun and put it on the pegs over the fireplace. "It won't shoot without shells," he told her. "And I keep them all in my pocket." Then his scowl darkened and he asked, "You seen anything of Graben?"

"No, I ain't!" she said. "But I was hopin' he'd come while you were gone. I meant to go with him if he'd let me."

Unger clenched his big fists and started toward her, then stopped and got himself under control, his chest rising and falling with his heavy breathing. His voice was hoarse and unsteady when he spoke. "Get a fire goin' and cook some supper. You ain't goin' nowhere. If you do I'll come after you and make you wish you hadn't. As for Graben, he'll be dead by the end of the week."

"Hah! I don't think he'll ever be dead. Not if you have to kill him. All of you put together ain't man enough to get him."

Just then Astin and Kester came in, and she asked, "Where are the others?"

It was Astin who answered. "Graben killed Zeke, and Knell stayed to hunt Graben's trail. That's what he said anyway. But if you ask me, he's got something else in mind."

Gibby looked at Unger. "Maybe you'd like to know why he came here? Well, I can tell you. It's because of me. My horse went lame on the way here from Turley's and I rode the rest of the way with Knell. That's the only reason he came back, to see me again. He ain't no outlaw!"

"What did you say?" Tobe Unger shouted hoarsely, his face turning purple with rage.

"You heard me!" she said and pointed at him. "Look at him! Boy, if you could see the look on your face!"

"Never mind that!" he roared. "I want to know what happened between you and that gunfighter!"

"Nothin' happened! That's just it! Nothin' at all happened and you're still goin' crazy with jealous rage!"

"How do I know nothin' happened? You've lied to me plenty of times before. How do I know you ain't lyin' now?"

"Why don't you ask Knell?" she taunted.

"I'm askin' you!"

"That's right," she said scornfully. "You're askin' me because you're scared to ask him!"

"We'll see about that!" Unger cried. "You just wait till he gets back!"

And striding to the fireplace, the big man took the double barrel shotgun down from its pegs and reloaded it.

"Ain't you afraid I might get my hands on that thing and use it on you?" Gibby sneered.

Dub Astin was looking out through the broken window. "Here comes Knell now."

Unger stepped over to the window and saw the lean dark rider coming unhurriedly down the trail.

The big man turned away from the window and growled orders. "Let's get ready! Barney, you set down in that chair over by the wall where Knell usually sets. Dub, you set at the table. I'll stay over here near the fireplace."

"I knew it," the girl said, smiling scornfully. "You're scared of him."

"I ain't scared," Unger said. "I just don't aim to lose."

CHAPTER 12

Knell left his horse saddled and ground-reined and stepped to the door of the shack. There he halted, letting his eyes adjust to the deeper gloom inside. The first thing he saw was the girl sitting in front of the broken window, and he suspected that she had been ordered to sit there on purpose, so his eyes would be on her when he came in and his face would give him away, if there was anything to give away. She seemed to be trying to warn him with her pale, frightened eyes, but the warning was unnecessary.

Kester sat over against the wall to his left, squirming in the chair where Knell had sat earlier. Dub Astin sat before him at the plank table, his hands out of sight below the table. Unger stood over near the fireplace wiping the sawed-off shotgun with a rag, the twin muzzles turned toward the door as if by accident and the rag hiding the hammers so that Knell could not tell whether they were cocked or not. In the dim shadowy light it would have been hard to tell anyway. He could not watch them all at once, spaced out as they were, and he knew that was the idea.

He came in a little farther into the room, moving away from the door to avoid being outlined against the fading light, and spoke casually, as if he suspected nothing wrong. "I didn't find his trail. It was getting a little dark to look for tracks on that hard ground."

"I could of told you that," Unger snorted. He scowled at Knell in silence for a moment, and then said, "Gibby says you gave her a ride after her horse went lame. She says that's the only reason you came back—to see her."

Knell glanced at the girl. "It was a natural assumption on her part," he said almost gently, as if not wishing to offend her. "She's a mighty pretty girl, and a lot of men would risk their necks just to get another look at her. But I'm not one of them."

"You ain't?"

Knell shook his head. "I came back because I thought you boys might be going after a bank or stage before long, and I can use a share of the money."

Unger bared his teeth in a savage grin. "She also said you wasn't no outlaw."

"I never said I was," Knell replied. "But I've done things I'd just as soon not talk about. Times are getting hard, and a man has to make a living anyway he can."

Unger scowled. "Looks like you've got all the answers," he said. "And I reckon you'll have one to why you rode over Graben's trail without sayin' anything. I don't mean the last time that you told us about. I mean the time before that when you didn't say nothin'."

Knell slowly nodded, glancing at Dub Astin. "I went on because I figured Graben was down there somewhere watching me. I meant to double back through the rocks, but then Barney started screaming like he'd been stuck and said Graben was already gone."

"Funny you didn't mention it after you knew he was gone," Unger said, still sounding suspicious and unconvinced.

"I didn't see any point in mentioning it then," Knell said simply.

Unger and Astin exchanged a silent look. After a time Astin shifted in his chair and said reluctantly, "Sounds like he might be tellin' the truth, Tobe. When he went on past the trail like that 'cause he thought Graben might be watchin' him, hell, I might of done the same thing in his place. I prob'ly would of."

Even Barney Kester nodded silent agreement. But Unger still was not satisfied, and his lingering scowl showed it. "All right, Knell," he said grudgingly. "But you better watch yoreself."

"I intend to," Knell said. He yawned and stretched sleepily. "I guess I'll bed down out in the brush. I've got so I can't sleep in a house." His glance took in the three watching outlaws. "And I don't think any of us would get much sleep if I stayed in here tonight."

Unger nodded, sharing the opinion. "We'll be leavin' at first light," he said. "Better get here early if you want any breakfast."

Knell left without answering. He avoided looking at Gibby Tate as he turned through the doorway, but he knew she was watching him with her strange pale eyes. A beautiful girl, he thought, but there was something wrong about her. Something twisted. She did not seem to know what she wanted, and would probably never be satisfied with whatever she had.

He let his horse drink at the waterhole, drank some of the warm muddy-looking water himself, and filled his canteen, keeping one eye on the shack. No one came outside, but he had a feeling they were watching him through the window, and he knew they would not light a lamp or start a fire until they saw him leave. It brought back an old feeling of loneliness, but he was relieved that he would be able to spend the night by himself away from the shack.

If they let him go. There was a chance that they might still try to prevent him from leaving. Tom and Frank Graben had both been shot, on separate occasions, as they tried to leave here, and Tobe Unger had just as much reason to want Knell dead, for it was clear that the big man no longer trusted him, if he ever had.

Knell knew they were watching to see if he unsaddled and put his horse in the corral with the others, which would have been proof that he was not leaving for good or going far during the night. But he had no intention of putting his horse in the corral, and he did not intend to leave by the main trail where his back would have been to the door as he rode away. Nor did he intend to go back past the shack door and take the trail that led toward Radner Canyon.

Instead he led his horse up through the rocks behind the waterhole, keeping the horse between himself and the shack until he was over the crest of the hill. This did not prove that he was smarter than the Graben brothers. He had merely learned from their mistake. He knew what to expect.

Inside the shack, Dub Astin stepped away from the window and holstered his gun, letting out a long breath. "Ain't he the careful one!" He pronounced it "keerful."

Unger stood near the door with the shotgun, his hands shaking a little, his big chest swelled up with tension. His shaggy head was bare. He had been waiting for Knell to come back from the waterhole and turn along the trail that led to the old shack at the crossroads, the logical place for him to spend the night. They did not believe what he had said about not being able to sleep inside a house. There were men like that and they had known some, but he did not look like the type to sleep on the ground by choice. He was too careful about his appearance, for one thing. It was possible, on the other hand, that he might prefer the ground to their company.

"I guess he figgered we'd shoot him in the back," Unger said, as he unloaded the shotgun and returned it to the pegs over the fireplace.

"Well, weren't you?" the girl asked.

Unger scowled at her. "You get a fire started and cook some supper," he said. "I don't aim to tell you again."

"I wish you'd make up your mind!" she said, getting angrily to her feet. "I already started to once and you told me to wait."

"I didn't want no light in my eyes till I made sure he was gone," Unger growled.

"You mean till you got a chance to shoot him in the back!"

"Look who's talkin'!" Unger sneered. "Crazy Cora's daughter!"

On the far side of the rocky hill, Mark Knell stepped into the saddle and walked his tired horse across the darkening desert toward the old shack at the crossroads. He was not surprised when he saw the two horses in the coral, and he did not change his pace or his direction. He rode into the yard at a shuffling walk and halted in front of the shack, looking straight ahead and remaining in the saddle, with the shack to his right where anyone could see the gun in his holster and watch his gun hand.

"Careless," he said quietly, "you being here."

"Not as careless as you riding up like that."

The voice came from the dark empty window to his right, but he did not look in that direction. Slowly, he put his right hand up to adjust his hat. A cool wind came in off the desert, blowing dust in his face. Wind and dust didn't bother Knell. It was people who worried him.

"Better leave it on."

"I meant to." He slowly brought his hand down and rested it on the saddle horn. "I knew Frank Graben," he said. "Or I should say I saw him once or twice. I was even mistaken for him a time or two. Not that we looked that much alike. It was more the way we dressed, and we were about the same size."

The quiet hard voice at the dark window hole did not change. "Anything else?"

"That's about it. I just thought I'd tell you."

"You've told me."

Knell nodded and lifted the reins. "You better watch out for Mac and Hump Radner," he said as a casual afterthought. "They'll be looking for you. And they may not be with the rest of us."

"Us?"

Again he nodded. "I'll be with them. But I wouldn't worry too much about it if I were you."

"I never worry."

Knell had nothing more to say. In silence he turned his horse and rode back the way he had come, and the man at the window did not try to stop him.

Tom Graben listened to the sound of the walking horse slowly fade away into the silence of the desert. Then he holstered his gun and returned to his blankets on the floor on the corner. As Knell had said, it was careless for him to be here. But he doubted if Unger and the others would think to look for him here, and somehow he did not believe Knell would tell them.

But after lying there for a few minutes he got to thinking about it. In his time he had trusted very few people, and usually they had turned out to be the very last ones he should have trusted. And what did he know about Knell? He did not even know if that was his name. He had just heard about him from time to time and figured it was probably him, although it might be someone else. It might be almost anyone.

But even if it was Knell, Graben still did not know much about him. Just vague rumors that had left him more puzzled than anything else. No one seemed to know much about the man and he apparently never bothered to enlighten anyone about himself or his past. Some said he had been an outlaw, others thought he had been some kind of lawman at one time. All agreed that he was quick and deadly with a gun, although few people had actually seen him use one. Few who were still alive anyway.

Once in a restaurant in Santa Fe Graben had heard some men at the counter discussing Knell, and the fat gossipy woman behind the counter had said, "They say when you see that man comin', you better watch out. Death ain't never far behind." Graben had thought for a moment that they were talking about him, but then he had heard Knell's name mentioned, so he supposed they were talking about Knell. "They say it's like a warnin' when you see him," the waitress had added.

Was that what Knell had been trying to do, warn him? In fact he had warned him about Mac and Hump Radner, and now Graben thought about them. They were part Indian and would probably be like Indians on a trail. They might even be able to track him by moonlight. It had been done before. Graben himself had done it a few times.

Moonlight hell, he thought. They could have tracked him most of the way here before dark, when it came to that. But that would have taken some doing, and he did not think there was much danger yet for a while. The moon had not yet risen, and even when it did, tracking by its uncertain light over hard rocky ground would be no easy matter even for them. There was a chance, of course, that they might guess where he was, as Knell had apparently done, but that was unlikely. They would be thinking of the places they might go if it were them, and this was probably about the last place they would go if men were on their trail.

But the uneasiness remained, and Graben knew he would get no sleep here tonight—and sleep was something he badly needed if he was to be fresh and alert tomorrow. Being fresh and alert might mean the difference between life and death.

Throwing the blanket aside, he rose and went to each glassless window hole in turn to peer out. There was no window in one wall but he could look out through the cracks between the logs. Like Crazy Cora's shack, this one was almost entirely surrounded by low rocky hills. But beyond the hills for a stretch in every direction there was relatively flat, open desert, broken by a few low ridges and dry sandy washes or arroyos.

He saw no sign of anyone in the rocks, and the two horses in the corral did not seem to share his uneasiness. He had watered them earlier in the ravine below the mesa, and after rubbing them down good and putting them in the corral he had given them a little grain. They needed rest and he hated to put them back to work so soon, but it had to be done.

Wasting no time he saddled up and a short time later he topped the rocky hill behind the shack and looked out across the desert toward the broken country beyond. He wanted to be back in the rough country before the moon rose, but to get there he had to cross that open stretch of desert that worried him. Yet there was no avoiding it, and after a moment he rode down through the rocks and started out across the flat.

The wind whipped dust into his slitted eyes and obscured his vision. He was wearing Frank's corduroy coat, but the chill soon penetrated it. By the calendar it was spring, and the days were hot enough for summer, but the nights were unpleasantly cold.

He suddenly got the feeling someone was watching him, and he glanced sharply about, then turned his head to look back at the rocky hill he had just left. He saw no sign of anyone, yet the feeling remained, so strong that he wanted to leap from the saddle to avoid the risk of a bullet in the back. Instead he bent low in the saddle and put his horses into a rapid canter across the desert.

No shots were fired, nothing happened, and he soon slowed to a trot, feeling like a fool. But even so he could not get rid of the notion that someone was watching him, and the feeling remained until he was out of the open desert and into the broken hilly country beyond.

As the moon rose he halted on the rough slope above the trail where Frank had been shot, near where he himself had stood and dispatched two of the shooters. When he opened fire he had not known for certain that the man slumped on the saddle was Frank. There had been no sure way to tell from where he stood, yet he had a strong feeling that it was his brother, and he had been right.

What had caused the feeling? Something familiar about the man that his subconscious mind had identified, even though he could not see his face? Or had it been something else? He had no way of knowing, but he would always wonder, just as he would wonder about a lot of things that had happened lately.

Like that feeling back there that someone was watching him. Nine out of ten people would probably say it was just his imagination, but in his own mind he would always believe someone had been watching him.

Had it been Knell? Or . . . ? He shook his head at the thought, and rode on down off the slope and across the trail where Frank had been shot, and up into the bleak eroded hills beyond.

As he rode he found himself remembering something he had seen in the old shack before it got dark. It was a spot on the ceiling, made by the saw cutting through a knot on one of the planks. But from a certain angle it had looked like the crude outline of a man's face, and once or twice it had looked to him like a distorted likeness of Frank's face, looking down at him and smiling a mocking smile.

Had he only imagined the face and the mocking smile because of a guilty conscience? The years had long since erased from his own mind any trace of bitterness he might have ever felt toward his brother, leaving only a feeling of regret that he himself had once been so young and stupid. But he did not know how Frank had felt about it, and he had often thought he should look him up and make things right. But he had always been a little afraid that they would get to arguing again and discover that nothing had really changed between them, and that they had only become more stubborn and set in their ways as they got older.

When he was approaching the cave at the foot of the mesa, Graben noticed that the blue roan, now carrying the pack started behaving in a peculiar manner. He began snorting and pointing his ears toward the cave, and tried once to wheel aside, then tried to jerk the lead rope out of Graben's hand and race on ahead.

As they got closer, an unmistakable stench of rotting flesh assailed Graben's nostrils, and it seemed to come from the cave. He thought he knew what he would find inside, and a cold chill went down his spine. He was almost afraid to look, but knew he had to.

When he got inside he struck a match and saw Frank sitting propped up against the wall of the cave. He was dead, but it was Frank, and there was a bullet hole between his eyes that had not been there when Tom had buried him.

That seemed to rule out Gibby Tate, who did not have a gun, but he thought he knew who had done this.

The Radners! It was almost as if they were saying to him, "We found your brother and put a bullet in him, and we'll do the same for you!"

CHAPTER 13

Tom Graben normally was a man who had absolute control of himself, but now he was shaking with cold rage, not to mention being a little unnerved at finding his dead brother sitting there like that in the dark cave.

Yet he knew this was no time to lose control of himself. If the Radners had opened the grave and brought Frank's body here, that meant they were already looking for him, Tom Graben, and might still be around somewhere.

The match had gone out and he stood there in the dark near the dead man, trying to blot out of his mind the way the partially decayed face looked with the little hole between the eyes and the face blackened by powder burns. The bullet had been fired from very close range, perhaps from no farther away than Tom was now standing. He knew they had done this not just to let him know what he could expect himself, but also to make him wild with bitterness and rage, and so angry that he would abandon all caution and do something reckless and crazy.

And that was exactly what he wanted to do. He wanted to go charging blindly after them in the dark, ignoring all thought of danger. But he knew that was just what they wanted. That would be to rush into the trap they had no doubt set for him, and it would almost certainly get him killed.

Worst of all, they would get away with what they had done, and it was this thought that made Tom Graben get hold of himself.

He was gripping a gun in his hand, and now he moved away from the corpse and stood near the mouth of the cave, peering out while his breathing and the beating of his heart gradually slowed back to normal. The two horses were just outside the cave where he had left them, the blue roan's lead rope securely tied to the horn of the saddle on the buckskin. The roan had quieted down and the buckskin never got excited unless he sensed danger. Now the gelding stood half asleep over the dropped reins, a fairly reliable indication that there was no one around. And since the Radners had no way of knowing when Graben would return to the cave, if at all, it seemed unlikely that they would have waited for him. And if they had, they would have probably been inside the cave and fired at him as he rode up.

Yet Graben could not be sure what they might do. It would never have occurred to him that they might dig up the body of his dead brother just to spite him. If they had done that, they might do almost anything.

So he waited there in the dark near the mouth of the cave with the gun in his hand and watched and listened, keeping one eye on the buckskin for any warning of danger. Below the cave the ground sloped down to the ravine about a hundred yards away. Between him and the ravine there were only a few scattered rocks and some low stunted brush, not much cover for an ambusher. Beyond the ravine there were larger rocks and boulders and buttes and barren eroded ridges dotted with cedars. It was that area that worried Graben at the moment, for there were a thousand places over there where an ambusher might lie in wait with a rifle and open up on him when he came out of the cave.

But to remain here was to run the risk of being trapped here. And he would be harder to hit in the dark than in the daylight, so the sooner he got away from here the better.

He hated to leave Frank's body there like that, but he did not see much point in burying him again, not now anyway. Mac and Hump Radner would probably just follow his tracks to the new grave and dig the body up again to spite him.

The bitter rage threatened to take possession of him again. It was not enough that Frank was dead. They could not even let his corpse rest in peace. Tom had never heard of anything like this before, and he had never known anyone whose mind was sick and twisted enough to conceive of such a thing. In some way, this seemed far worse to him and unsettled him more than Frank's murder had, and he did not intend to show these perpetrators any more mercy when he found them.

But in one way his mind was more at peace now, for he knew the living had nothing to fear from the dead. If anything, it was the other way around.

Frank could not do anything about the treatment he had received, but Tom could do something about it, and he fully intended to.

But he would not be able to do anything about it if he got himself killed first.

He checked his guns in the dark, kept one in his hand, and eased out to the horses, watching the rocks and shadows on the far side of the ravine. Nothing happened and he stepped into the saddle and turned along the foot of the mesa, keeping to the shadows under the mesa wall.

He thought of his dead brother back there in the cave, and his heart was heavy and filled with bitterness and hatred for Frank's killers and for those who wouldn't let him rest in peace. Don't worry, he thought. I'll make them pay, every mother's son of them, if I can just last long enough.

It had not occurred to him to look for tracks outside the cave. Even in the daylight it would have been a difficult task on that hard rocky ground. And here in the shadows where he rode now it would certainly be a waste of time.

In any case, he did not intend to try to trail the men who had dug Frank up and put him in the cave. There were safer, if not quicker, ways to find them. He knew who they were and where to watch for them. And even if he was wrong about who they were, it did not matter, because the men he intended to look for were men he would have to kill anyway or they would kill him. This was war and from now on he intended to shoot first and talk later.

He had intended to find a place to sleep, but now he knew that sleep was out of the question. Finding Frank in the cave had left him feeling the same way he had felt the night he had buried him, tormented in mind and body and seething with cold rage in spite of himself.

Well, he thought, if I can't get any sleep, I don't know why the hell I should let them get any. And turning his horses he rode to the rocky hill above Crazy Cora's shack and dismounted.

As he drew his gun he thought about Knell and felt a sudden irritation at the man. He had no wish to fight the man and had the feeling that Knell had no wish to fight him either. But as long as he was with Unger and the others, it would be hard to fight them without fighting him also.

"The hell with him," Graben muttered, and cocking the long-barreled Colt he emptied it at the shack in one angry burst of firing. "Wake up, you sons of bitches!" he roared as he reloaded. "If you're looking for me, here I am! Anybody down there don't want to fight get the hell out! And keep out of my way! Anybody comes hunting me will get some lead!"

Those in the shack were flat on the floor and the three men were gripping revolvers in their hands. Knell had not returned. The girl was a dim shape near the bed. Dub Astin began crawling toward the broken window. Tobe Unger and Barney Kester remained where they were, tensely listening, and both ducked and flinched when another stream of bullets thudded into the logs.

"He's just wastin' lead," Dub Astin said almost casually. "Be a pure accident if—"

Just then a bullet shattered another pane of the window and showered him with broken glass. He grunted and scrambled to one side.

Barney Kester laughed shrilly. "What was you just sayin'?"

"Shut up, you little bastard."

Kester laughed again, but said nothing more.

"Barney," Tobe Unger said after a moment.

"Oh no you don't!" the little man whined. "Whatever you got in mind, Dub can do it this time! I'm tired of you pickin' on me!"

Tobe's narrowed eyes went toward the little man in the dark. "You ain't as big as he is, and it will be harder for Graben to see you in the dark. You can sneak out the door, circle around and crawl up through the rocks without him ever seein' you, if you're careful."

"Oh no!" Barney said. "I ain't about to!"

"You'll do whatever I tell you," Unger said savagely, gripping his big Remington. "If you don't do what I say, I'll put a slug in you myself."

"Ain't you forgettin' something?" Kester cried in a trembling voice. "I got a gun too, and you make a lot bigger target in the dark than I do!"

Dub Astin waited curiously to see what Unger would do, but Unger was silent and motionless, apparently thinking over what Barney had said.

"Hell, Tobe, Graben will probably be gone time he gets up there," Astin said to break the tension. "He may be gone already. He knows better than to hang around up there with Mac and Hump Radner huntin' him."

Gibby Tate spoke up then. "Why don't you go, Tobe? Show us all what a big tough man you are. But you ain't so big and tough unless you're pickin' on somebody about half your size, are you?"

"You shut up!" he told her.

Just then Tom Graben's voice rang out again. "What's wrong, Unger? You ain't scared, are you?"

"Why don't you try tellin' him to shut up?" the girl asked.

Unger scowled at her in the dark, but said nothing.

"Yeah he's scared!' the girl called. "He's just a great big coward! He won't fight nobody but women and runts half his size!" Then she added, "He tried to send Barney up after you!"

"You shouldn't send a little runt to do a big man's job, Unger!" Graben called back. "Why not come yourself?"

"That's all right, Graben!" the big man shouted. "We'll get you soon enough!"

"We?" Graben taunted. "Ain't you got guts enough to try it by yourself?"

Unger did not answer, and after a little silence Graben yelled, "If you see the Radners before I do, tell them the happy hunting ground ain't what it's cracked up to be! Tell them they'll find my brother waiting there for them, when I get done with them!"

"What's he mean by that?" Dub Astin asked, but no one answered. Gibby Tate shifted in her corner, but remained silent. After a time Astin spoke again. "He must of left, or we'd of heard something else out of him by now."

Unger crawled over to the broken window and peered out, then got slowly to his feet.

"We better watch out, Barney," Gibby Tate said. "If Graben's gone, Tobe will set in on you and me and take it out on us. He knows better than to bother anyone else."

Unger scowled at her, but said nothing.

"You goin' after him, Tobe?" Dub asked.

"If we couldn't track him when it was light, how can we in the dark?" Unger growled, putting away his gun and going back toward the bed.

"He's scared," the girl said, getting to her feet.

Unger swung his big hand and knocked her back down. He pointed his finger at her and cried hoarsely, "Now you shut up!"

"Hell, there ain't no need to take it out on her, Tobe," Astin said.

"He takes everything out on me!" the sobbing girl said bitterly. "Why I came back here I'll never know. I must be crazy as Mama was."

Unger snorted scornfully. "That old bitch was smart compared to you! She had enough brains to keep her mouth shut, till the mornin' I shot her!"

Mark Knell heard the shooting and guessed what was happening. When the shooting stopped, he tried again to get some sleep, but could not even get drowsy. He had not slept well in years. If he managed to sleep a few hours during the night he considered himself lucky.

He wanted a cigarette, but was afraid it might be seen glowing in the dark. He had bedded down in some brush and rocks about a half mile from the shack, and his horse was staked nearby on a little patch of dead grass that entirely hid the new grass underneath. In this country it was hard to tell when spring came. It always looked like fall or winter—everything gray and dead-looking except for the stunted cedars that were always green. But the country suited his mood, which was also gray and bleak. He had an uneasy feeling that he belonged in some godforsaken place like this, whether he liked it or not.

He thought of Tom Graben, a man who was a lot like himself in some ways. They were both loners. Frank Graben had also been a loner, and a lot like Tom, yet different. Some of the world's callousness had rubbed off on Frank and as a result he had thought less of the world and of himself. A man somehow tarnished, from all accounts he had behaved at times as if he were trying to get himself killed, and had feared only one thing—that he might not be able to take his killers with him.

Which was the way it had worked out. But it appeared now that he need not have worried about that. Tom Graben was just as good with a gun as Frank had been, and he had made his intentions abundantly clear. Most of those who had shot Frank were already dead, and Dub Astin, the only one left, was just marking time, whether he knew it or not.

Astin was one of those likable, mild-mannered fellows who would grin at you and then shoot you in the back when you turned to walk away. He and the others had already done that to Tom Graben, so Tom had his own personal score to settle with them, aside from what had happened to Frank.

It was beginning to look like Tom would not need any help, but Knell wanted to be on hand just in case.

In the meantime perhaps he could do Graben a small favor. Since it did not look like he was going to get any sleep anyway, he could see that Tobe Unger and the others did not get any sleep either.

Leaving his horse where it was, he walked back toward the shack, but circled and came up from the back side of the rocky hill where Graben had been. He glanced at the moon, judged the time, and waited a while. Then he slipped his gun out of the holster and began firing.

In the shack, Tobe Unger, just getting drowsy after the previous excitement, gave a hoarse cry of rage and rolled out of the bed. Dub Astin groaned in dismay and sat up rubbing his eyes. The girl sat up in bed and angrily hugged her knees. Barney Kester, standing guard at the window, cried out as he jumped back and clawed at his face where the flying glass had cut him.

"You all right, Barney?" Dub asked.

"No, I ain't all right!" the little man screamed.

"I only ast."

"I'm cut!" Barney cried, looking at the blood on his hand. "My face is bleedin'!"

"Oh, shut up," Gibby Tate said. "Stop whinin' every little thing happens."

"Every little thing! I'd like to know—"

"Shut up!" Tobe Unger roared. "Both of you!"

"You goin' after him this time, Tobe?" Dub Astin said in his unexcitable drawl.

"You too!" Unger cried, holding his head in his hands. "All of you shut up and let me think! It ain't enough I got Graben up there! I got all you crazy bastards in here!"

Mark Knell stood in the cold wind on the rocky hill and calmly thumbed fresh shells into the loading gate of his gleaming dark pistol, the faint suggestion of a smile on his lips.

Tom Graben stepped out from behind a rock with a gun in his hand. "Knell, what the hell are you doing here?" he asked. "What's your game anyway?"

"No game," Knell said, glancing around. "I just like to see people get what they've got coming to them."

"The world is full of deserving folks," Graben said. "You don't have to poach on my territory. Go find your own."

Knell dropped his gun back into the holster and looked at the tall man uncertainly. "I didn't know you were still around," he said.

"I was waiting for them to get sleepy," Graben said. "I was just going to wake them up again when you showed up and spoiled my fun."

"I couldn't sleep and it didn't seem right for them to," Knell said. "But I've noticed that people whose conscience should keep them awake usually sleep like babies while I lie awake listening to them snore. When I heard you blasting away up here it gave me an idea. But I hadn't meant to tell anyone about it." He was silent for a moment, frowning. "I just thought of something."

"What's that?"

"I seem to be doing a lot of talking lately. I must be getting old."

"Me too," Graben said, watching him with cold eyes. "I've been doing a lot of gabbing lately myself, when I probably should of been shooting."

"Well, since you're still on the job here, I guess I'll just run along," Knell said.

"You do that," Graben told him. "In fact, I think it would be a good idea for you to ride on."

Knell had started walking away, but now he paused to look back at Graben. "I just thought of a story I once heard about Frank Graben," he said.

"Oh?"

"Seems he told somebody only one thing really bothered him, and it was that when he cashed in, whoever got him might live to brag about it."

"They won't brag long," Tom Graben said. "Some of them have already quit bragging."

"What if the others get you?" Knell asked. "What if they get you before you get them? Have you got any more brothers?"

"No," Graben said. After a moment he asked, "Did you hear any more stories about Frank?"

Knell hesitated. "Maybe it would be better if you just remembered him the way he used to be."

"Did the world rub off on him?"

"I sort of gathered that."

"Well, it's rubbed off on all of us," Tom said. "You too, I guess."

"The world doesn't bother me," Knell said. "It's the people in it."

"That's what I meant," Graben said. He was silent for a moment, looking down toward Crazy Cora's shack. "Why did you ask if I had any more brothers?"

"If they kill you too, I was just wondering who'll finish squaring things for you and Frank," Knell said.

"I don't guess anybody will."

"Somebody will," Knell said as he walked away.

Chapter 14

Dub Astin checked his gun in the dark and said, "I been thinkin', Tobe. He must be aimin' to stay up there and keep us awake the rest of the night."

"You think I ain't thought of that?" Unger growled.

"I been thinkin' about what you said earlier," Astin said. "About somebody sneakin' up there."

"Don't remind him!" Barney Kester said. "He'll be tryin' to send me again."

"I was thinkin' about goin' with you, Barney," Astin said. "Two would stand a lot better chance than one."

"Oh no," Barney said. "I ain't goin' unless we all go, and that includes Tobe!"

Unger scowled murderously at him, but said nothing.

"I got a idea," Gibby Tate said suddenly.

She was sitting on the bed, and the three men turned their heads to peer at her pale hair and the dim outline of her face in the dark.

"I could go," she said. "I could walk right up that hill and he wouldn't shoot me."

"Why should he?" Unger snorted.

"Wait a minute, Tobe," Astin said. "Let's hear what she's got to say."

"I could wear my white dress so he'll know it's me," she said. "And I could hide a gun in my—"

Unger again snorted his derision. "You must think I'm crazy! I ain't about to let you have no gun! You'd prob'ly try to use it on me!"

"Tom Graben killed my mama," she said in a trembling voice. "I want him dead just as much as you do."

Unger shook his head, refusing to consider it.

"Wait a minute, Tobe," Astin said. "We might have something here that'll work."

"What makes you think she'll use the gun on him even if we give her one?" Unger asked. "It's prob'ly just a trick she's thought up to get away from me and go back off with him!"

"But think about it for a minute, Tobe," Astin said. "What if she's on the level? How can we afford to pass up a chance like this? If we go after him ourselves, some more of us are gonna die before we get him. And how many of us are left now? Just you and me and Barney. We can't count on Knell. He's liable to turn that gun on us before it's over. I say we give Gibby a gun and let her go up there. Graben won't shoot her and he won't be expectin' her to shoot him, if she keeps the gun out of sight till she gets ready to use it."

Unger looked at the girl. "I don't trust her," he said. "I never saw a woman yet I could trust, and she's worse than most. Even if she aims to go through with it now, she may change her mind when she gets up there."

"Tobe! What choice have we got? It may be our only chance to come out of this alive."

"He ain't worried about nobody but hisself," Gibby Tate said. "He can always find some more men to boss around. The only one he can't replace is hisself, and he'll make sure he comes out alive if nobody else does."

"You ain't bein' fair neither, Gibby," Astin said. "Tobe's been takin' just as many chances as the rest of us."

"Oh no he ain't!" Barney Kester said. "I been takin' more than anybody, 'cause he made me! Now my face is all cut 'cause he had me standin' over there at that winder—"

"Oh, be quiet," Gibby Tate said. "I get so tired of hearin' you whine about everything. Worse than a baby."

"No worse than you!"

Ignoring him, she turned to Unger. "Are you goin' to let me or not, Tobe? Like Dub says, it may be your only chance to come out of this alive."

Unger sat scowling at her and working his dark brows like a man wrestling with a problem he could not solve.

Then he suddenly got up, strode to the broken window and roared, "You wanted this crazy girl, Graben! All right, you can have her! She's comin' out! I got no more use for her!"

Tom Graben was so surprised that he did not answer. He thought it must be some kind of trick, and he watched the shack with a sharper attention and listened for any sound. But it was strangely silent down there following the angry roar of Tobe Unger's bull voice, and he saw no sign of the girl Unger had said was coming out.

When she finally came around the corner of the house in a white dress that seemed to glow in the dark, his first impulse was to tell her to get back inside, he had no use for her either. But then it occurred to him that if he sent her back and she got shot by mistake, he would always blame himself. He did not know how things would work out and this might be her last chance to get away from Tobe Unger. Maybe she had finally learned her lesson, though he doubted it.

"Don't shoot, Graben!" she called. "I'm comin' up!"

He did not answer. He was still by no means convinced that this was not a trick of some kind. And as she came unhurriedly up the slope, he paid less attention to her than to the rocks and shadows on either side of the shack. For one of the men might try to circle around and sneak up on him while the girl had his attention.

She came slowly and silently toward him through the rocks, never taking her eyes off his face. When she was no more than eight feet away she stopped and brought the gun from behind her back and pointed it at him.

"Mine's cocked," Graben told her.

In the darkness she and not noticed that the gun in his hand was pointed directly at her, for she was still looking up at the shadow of his face under his hat brim.

She handed her own gun to him and said, "Take me with you, Graben. I just got to get away from Tobe and them. They're drivin' me crazy."

He shook his head, ramming her gun in his belt. "You wouldn't be any better off with me than with them. Either way you stand to catch a stray bullet. But if you want to hide out for a while, maybe I can get hold of a horse for you to get out of the country on. That's what you should have done instead of going back down there."

"Tobe took that hundred dollars you give me," she said bitterly. "Now I don't know what I'll do."

"That don't surprise me," he said, looking down toward the shack. "Did he give you that gun and send you up here to kill me?"

"That was my idea," she said. "I figured it was the only way to get away. But I never meant to shoot you any of the time."

"Why's it so quiet down there?" Graben asked. "They all out of ammunition?"

"They're scared to get near that winder," she told him. "You shot out another pane of glass a little while ago. Barney Kester got his face cut, and he's been whinin' about it ever since."

Graben grinned at the thought of Barney Kester with his face cut and whining about it. He took a tentative aim at the dull glint of the broken window, wondering if he could duplicate Knell's shot in the dark. Then he changed his mind, turned the gun toward the remote sky, and flame leapt from the muzzle.

Startled by the loud roar, the girl asked, "What did you do that for?"

Graben replaced the spent shell, glancing at her with hard eyes. "They're down there waiting for you to shoot me," he said. "Why don't you call down there and tell them it's safe to come on up now."

She gaped at him. "You mean it?"

He nodded. "Go ahead."

She hesitated, then took a deep breath and yelled down the slope, her voice shrill with excitement, almost hysterical. "Y'all can come on up now! He's dead!"

There followed a tense, uneasy silence. Graben waited with his gun ready, watching the shack, but aware that the pale-haired girl was watching him.

Then Tobe Unger shouted through the dark broken window, "I don't trust you, you bitch! It could be a trick for all I know! You come on back down here and bring his guns with you! And his shirt—and there better be some blood on it!"

Before Graben could think of any new instructions, Gibby Tate yelled back, "The hell with you, Tobe Unger! I ain't never comin' back down there! I'll just get on his horse and ride on off! That's what I meant to do anyway!"

"You better not pull that!" The big man's angry voice shook like thunder. "I'll come after you and make you wish you'd never been born!"

"I'm goin'!" she answered, and started on up through the rocks.

"Where do you think you're going?" Graben asked softly.

"I better make out like I'm leavin'," she said. "They can prob'ly see this white dress. It shines like a lantern."

"Do whatever you like," Graben told her. "Just don't go looking for my horses."

"Gibby!" Tobe Unger roared.

Graben saw her pale head turn as she yelled back, "Ah, shut up!" Then she giggled and said softly, "I been wantin' to tell him that for a long time now."

From the shack came Unger's hoarse cry of rage. "You just wait till I get my hands on you!"

"You'll never get your filthy hands on me again, you bastard!" she yelled back. Then she added, "You make me sick!"

"You stay right where you are!" Unger told her. "I'm comin' up there, and you better be there when I get there!"

"Come ahead!" she replied. Then she added maliciously, looking at Graben, "If you want a bullet!"

"Shut up," he grunted.

"He'll think I meant I'll shoot him myself," she said.

Just then Unger called, as if to prove what she had just said, "You try usin' that gun on me, I'll make you wish you hadn't!"

A moment later Unger and the other two appeared at the corner of the shack and started up the slope like dark shadows.

"Looks like they fell for it," Graben muttered, squatting down behind a rock.

The girl stood watching them in silence, her breasts rising and falling as she breathed. Now, for the first time, she seemed really frightened.

"Better get behind a rock," Graben told her.

But she did not respond until Unger bellowed at her, almost as if he were countermanding Graben's quiet advice, even though he had not heard it. "You stay right where you are and don't move, Gibby! I got Crazy Cora's shotgun here and I'll use it if I have to!" Then she sank behind a rock.

"I'm warnin' you, Gibby!" Unger bawled. "You fire one shot and I'll splatter them rocks with buckshot!"

She let out a shrill laugh. "You better get back down that hill, Tobe Unger, if you know what's good for you! What makes you think I never tricked you? How do you know Graben ain't up here waitin' for you?"

"Be quiet, dammit!" Graben hissed at her.

But it was too late. Down near the foot of the slope, the three shadowy figures froze in their tracks, then darted for cover among the rocks.

"You'll pay for this, Gibby!" Unger cried hoarsely. "I knower all along it was a trick! But you just wait! After we get Graben, I'll tend to you!"

"You won't do nothin'!" she retorted. "If Graben don't kill you, I'll get hold of a gun and do it myself! You won't never be able to sleep for wonderin' if I'll put a bullet in you or stick a butcher knife between your ribs!"

"I'll worry about that later! Right now I got bigger fish to fry!" There was a moment of silence, and then Unger roared, "Graben!"

Graben made no reply.

"He's up here waitin' behind a rock to put a bullet in you!" Gibby Tate called cheerfully down the slope. "He just ain't sayin' nothin', so you'll think he's dead!"

"Shut up," Graben said again in a low voice.

But she ignored him. She was enjoying herself. "Just come on up now, Tobe, and see what happens! He'll blow your head off!"

"You get back down that hill," Graben said in a quiet, deadly tone. "I don't want you around me. Let Unger worry about you. You and him deserve each other."

"You must be crazy!" she exclaimed. "Anybody starts down that hill now will get shot!"

"That's too bad," he said. He raised his voice and called, "Unger! Your girl's coming back down! And you're welcome to her!"

"You get on back down here, Gibby!" was Unger's only reply.

"Not a chance!" she cried, and suddenly ran off through the rocks in the opposite direction.

Cussing softly, Graben started to go after her. But someone down the slope caught the shadowy movement as he started to rise and fired a shot at him. Ducking behind the rock, he fired back at the muzzle flash, and drew the angry fire of the other two. A heavy slug screamed off a nearby rock and buckshot rattled all around him.

Gibby Tate screamed, and for a moment Graben thought she had been stung by the buckshot. Then she yelled, "Graben! There's somebody over here!"

He threw a quick glance over his shoulder and saw her pale silhouette darting through the rocks in a new direction. Then lightening and thunder stabbed at him from a rock near where she had been a moment before. Behind the flash he caught a brief glimpse of a dark form but he could not see the man's face. The first person he thought of was Knell, but then he realized that it was probably one of the Radners. What a fool he had been to forget about them!

He snapped a shot that drove the man to cover, and then he heard feet pounding up the slope as Unger, Astin and Kester tried to narrow the distance between them and him. He threw a shot their way, then swung his gun back toward the man behind the rock as the man rose quickly to nail him. Graben squeezed the trigger but his gun merely clicked, not on an empty shell but on a bad one, a dud. He flung himself to one side as the other man fired. He heard the man's bullet whistle past his ear.

"Graben!" Gibby Tate screamed again. She was now too far away to be trying to warn him, so it must have been a cry for help. But he had his own worries.

Caught off balance with most of his weight on his left elbow, he tried to bring his gun to bear on the man behind the rock. But the man ducked from sight and bobbed up in a different place, firing rapidly at him. Hot lead burned the air all around him and one bullet nicked his hat.

Then his own gun exploded, and over the leaping dark barrel he saw the man driven back by the force of the bullet as if he had been struck a hard blow by an invisible fist. The man fell from sight behind the rock, and Graben turned his attention back down the slope toward Unger and the other two.

They had taken cover again in the rocks, although higher up the slope and closer to Graben, and now Unger bawled, "If you Radners are up there, one of you catch that crazy girl! Don't let her get away!"

There was no answer, and no further sound from Gibby Tate. She had faded from sight, had gotten away on foot or had been carried off by the other Radner brother. The one behind the rock was either dead or keeping mighty quiet.

"Mac! Mac Radner!" Unger roared. "Is that you and Hump up there?"

There was still no answer. Graben quietly reloaded his gun and checked the loads in the one he had taken from Gibby Tate. The gun seemed familiar. He was pretty sure it was Barney Kester's gun. Apparently the Unger bunch only had one handgun apiece, which was almost unheard of among outlaws, many of whom were walking arsenals.

Well, the less hardware they had, the better for Graben, and he decided to get the gun and ammunition that had belonged to the man behind the rock, to keep them from getting it after he was gone. Keeping low, he crawled over to the rock and peered around it.

But there was no one behind the rock, only some dark bloodstains on the ground where the wounded man had crawled off through the rocks.

CHAPTER 15

Graben knew it would be a risky business to go after the wounded man in the dark. The man might wait for him in the rocks and kill him when he approached. It would be better to wait until daylight. By then the man might die from his wound.

In any case, Graben still had Unger and those other two to worry about. Without exposing himself, he crawled away from the rock and again faced down the slope toward the shack. He saw a shadowy movement down there about sixty yards away and he stopped on all fours behind a stunted cedar to watch.

One of them was crawling silently up the slope toward him, moving cautiously from rock to rock.

Graben rested the long barrel of his .44 over a cedar limb and waited.

When the crawling man had closed the distance to fifty yards, Graben squeezed the trigger. The gun bucked and roared. The man screamed and scrambled behind a rock.

"I'm hit!" Barney Kester cried. "My arm's broke! I knew this would happen! But you said he wouldn't see me! Now my face is cut and my arm's broke and—"

"Shut up!" Tobe Unger roared, hoarse with rage and frustration.

"Now I'll prob'ly bleed to death!" the little man whined bitterly. "Or die of lead poisonin'! That kills a lot of men!"

"Dammit, I told you to shut up!" Unger's voice was even louder and more threatening than before. "I'm sick and tired of you whinin' and cryin' about everything."

"My arm's broke!" Barney Kester screamed back at him. "And it's all yore fault! You had to keep sendin' me every time when you was afraid to go yoreself! Well, you ain't sendin' me no more! I'm goin' back to the house!"

"It looks like we all might as well go back!" Unger cried. "If a little rat like you can't sneak up on him, two big lunks like me and Dub shore as hell can't! And I reckon them damn Radners got scared and run off with that crazy girl, instead of catchin' her for me!"

Tom Graben called down the slope in a taunting voice, "What's wrong, Unger? No guts?"

The big man's reply was a bellow of rage. "Don't worry, Graben! We'll get you soon enough!"

"It's always 'we'll get you,'" Graben said. "What are you going to do when it's down to just you and me, Unger? When there's nobody else left to send after me?"

Unger, surprisingly, was silent. It was Barney Kester, walking back down the slope in full view and holding his left arm in his good hand, who said over his shoulder, "Don't worry! He won't come after you by hisself! You'll have to come after him, and he'll be mighty hard to find!"

"You better git down, Barney!" Dub Astin called.

"Let the little fool get his head blowed off!" Unger growled. "You can't tell him nothin'! He accuses me of tryin' to get him killed, then he stands up where a blind man could see him and starts walkin' off like there wasn't a thing to worry about!"

"I can't crawl on a broke arm!" Barney cried.

"That arm ain't broke! If it was, you'd be squealin' like a stuck pig!"

"It sure feels broke! I can't hardly move it!"

"I bet it ain't hardly even scratched!" Unger snorted. "He thought he was bleedin' to death from that little scratch on his face!"

"How do you know how bad it is? You ain't even seen it!"

The little man stumbled on down the slope in plain view, and Graben could hear the other two crawling noisily back down through the rocks toward the shack.

"You boys ain't leaving, are you?" he called.

"We'll be down here at the shack, Graben, if you want anything!" Unger shouted. "Why don't you try comin' after us!"

"I may do that," Graben replied. "You boys better not get too comfortable down there. Somebody's liable to try to sneak up on you."

"Come ahead!" Unger told him. "We'll be waitin'!"

A little later, when they were back in the shack, Graben heard Barney Kester whine, "Oh no you don't! I ain't gettin' near that winder! I already got my face cut! Somebody else can stand guard the rest of the night!"

Graben grinned to himself and began moving off through the rocks. Then he remembered the wounded man and halted, looking uneasily in the direction he believed the man had gone. If the wounded man was still around, his brother was probably still around somewhere also. For Graben felt certain that the man behind the rock had been one of the Radners.

He didn't know what had happened to Gibby Tate and he didn't much care. She was more trouble than she was worth, and if the Radners had carried her off, they were welcome to her. She would bring them nothing but misery. Of course, it was possible that they intended to take her back to Tobe Unger the first chance they got. Provided they had her—it was just as possible that she had escaped alone. If so, she would not go far on foot.

A faint metallic ring came to Graben's ears—the unmistakable sound of a shod hoof on rock. He raised his head, listening. The sound was not repeated, but he was pretty sure it had come from the back side of the ridge and maybe a hundred yards to his right. There was a gully over there, winding down the slope through the rocks and brush, and he suspected that the Radners were quietly retreating along it, although one of them might still be around here somewhere, laying for him. He doubted that however, and after a time he began working his way carefully through the rocks toward his horses.

It was well past midnight when he got back to the spot where he had left the horses. The moon shed a pale frosty light on the rocks. The wind stirring through the stunted cedars had turned unpleasantly cold, although he had scarcely noticed the growing chill until now.

The horses, hidden in a pocket among the rocks, were just as he had left them. He checked the pack on the roan and tightened the buckskin's cinch, then stepped into the saddle. He did not start out at once. He sat there for a while thinking about the sound he had heard earlier, the ring of a shod hoof on rock. The gully where he believed the sound had come from was not far from here, just off down there a piece below him.

After a few minutes he picked his way through the rocks in that direction at a cautious walk. Before he got to the gully he dismounted, left his horses and went the rest of the way on foot. In the gully he found what he had expected to find, the tracks of two shod horses. On the hard ground the tracks were faint and barely invisible in the pale moonlight, but they were there. And a little farther down the gully he found a dark drop of blood on a rock. One of them was wounded and they had been traveling slowly and as quietly as possible, keeping their horses to a walk. With little doubt it was the Radners and they were probably headed for their shack in Radner Canyon, to do whatever could be done for the wounded man.

Graben's first impulse was to leave them alone for the time being. But something inside him immediately hardened against that thought. For he kept thinking about the way his dead brother had looked in the cave with the bullet hole between his eyes and the powder stains on his face. He also thought about the way the man behind the rock up there had kept shooting at him, evidently trying very hard to kill him. And he knew that if the man recovered from his wound he would be trying it again before long, and his brother would be helping him, both of them more determined than ever to kill Graben. If he showed them any mercy they would repay him with lead.

The thought turned Graben's eyes cold in the moonlight. He climbed out of the gully, went back to his horses and headed for Radner Canyon.

He rode at a fast trot and sometimes at a canter, hoping to reach the shack in the canyon before the Radners. But when he reined in on the rim and looked into the canyon, he saw a saddled horse standing in front of the dark shack. It looked to him like someone had got out of the saddle and gone inside, leaving the reins grounded and perhaps intending to come back out shortly and leave again. Graben decided to remain where he was and see which way the man went.

But after ten minutes he had seen no one come out of the shack, and he grew puzzled. The thought had entered his mind that one of the Radners might have come back for grub and a few necessities, intending to return to some hideout in the hills where he had left his wounded brother. But Graben began to doubt if this was the case, and to suspect that it was the wounded brother who had for some reason returned alone to the shack. The other one might have gone back to look for Graben, or he might have gone after a doctor.

When an hour had passed, Graben decided to take a look. He rode along the rim until he was almost to the gap where the trail ran down into the canyon. Then he left his horses tied in the rocks and went the rest of the way on foot, circling around behind the shack and slipping up to a rear window. The shack was dark but through the window he could see a man sitting slumped in a chair before the cold fireplace, his chin on his chest. The man appeared to be asleep or unconscious, perhaps even dead.

Graben went around to the front of the house and stepped in silently through the open door, a gun in his hand. The man in the chair did not move. Graben stepped up behind him, pressed the muzzle of his gun to the back of the man's neck and felt for the man's gun. But the man's holster was empty. He must have lost his gun somewhere en route, probably when he was crawling through the rocks, Graben thought.

The man stirred finally and grumbled, "What did you come back for? I already told you I don't know where Mac is. I ain't seen him since before I got shot. He must of gone chasin' off after that crazy girl."

"Wait a minute," Graben said, thinking the man must be half out of his head. "Didn't Mac come back with you, or at least part of the way?"

"I ain't seen Mac since me and him separated up on that ridge," Hump Radner said in a strange, hollow voice. "But I told you that when you was here earlier. What did you come back for? Can't a man die in peace in his own house?"

"You're out of your head," Graben told him. "I've never been here before in my life."

"Somebody sure was here," Hump Radner said. "Snuck up behind me and shoved a gun in my back before I knew anyone was around. Just like you. Asked about the same questions, too."

"What did he look like?" Graben asked.

"I couldn't tell. It was dark, and he stayed behind me."

Graben was silent for a moment, wondering if it could have been Knell. He could think of no one else that it could have been.

He noticed that Hump Radner's head had sunk back on his chest. "How bad are you hit?" he asked.

"Bad enough. I'm tryin' to last till Mac gets back, but he better hurry if he wants to find me alive." The man's tone was oddly matter-of-fact, with no emotion in it, except for a slight irritation at being kept waiting.

After a moment Graben asked, "Was it you boys who dug up my brother and put him in that cave?"

Hump Radner slowly shook his head. "We found him there and Mac shot him in the face because of what you done to Ed. But we never dug him up or brought him there. It was prob'ly that crazy girl."

"Gibby Tate?"

Hump Radner nodded his head, but more as if he had suddenly dozed off than in answer to the question.

"I think I know why she did it," Graben said, thinking of Crazy Cora. "Well, two can play her game. There's not much else anyone can do to Frank anyway. And what I've got in mind might even appeal to him, if he knew about it."

He was talking more to himself than to Hump Radner, and that was just as well, because Hump Radner was not listening. He had died there in the chair without a sound. When Graben tried to prod him awake, he fell out of the chair.

Graben bent down to make sure the man was dead, then straightened up and went to the door to look out. Hump Radner's saddled horse still stood patiently waiting before the shack, the reins hanging. Graben could see the dark shapes of other horses grazing on the other side of the canyon, near the wall. The pale moon was visible above the rim, outlining the rocks and the stunted cedars. The canyon bottom was carpeted with grass and spotted with brush, some of it sage.

He looked both ways along the canyon, his glance lingering on the notch in the wall where the trail was. He saw no sign of anyone, and after a moment he unsaddled the horse and turned it loose. Hump Radner would not need it anymore.

As he crossed the canyon floor and climbed out to the rim, Graben kept remembering what Hump Radner had said about the man who had been there earlier. It must have been Knell, but what had he wanted, and why had he asked about Mac Radner?

From the opposite rim, Mark Knell watched Graben cross the canyon floor and climb out of the canyon. After the man was gone, Knell took a chance and lit a thin cigar. Someone might spot the tiny red glow, but the odds were against it. Not that he really cared. If anyone wanted to come after him, he could easily be gone before they got here, or he could wait here in the rocks for them, whichever he chose.

He almost hoped Mac Radner would come after him. Graben would have his hands full with Unger, Astin and Kester. He did not need Mac Radner stalking him as well. In this kind of fight, a man like Mac would be more dangerous than those other three combined, although he probably wasn't any better with a gun.

And Mac would certainly be looking for Graben, now that Graben had killed Ed and Hump—if Hump was not dead by now, he was close to it. He had been only half conscious part of the time when Knell had dropped in on him earlier, and had seemed to think that he, Knell, was Graben. It was not the first time he had been mistaken for a Graben, Knell reflected.

He thought of Frank Graben, a man he had known briefly in New Mexico. He gathered that Frank had been the younger of the two brothers, yet in some ways he had looked older than Tom. There had been permanent squint wrinkles around his eyes and his face had been cured to old leather by the sun and wind. Even so, it would have been a strikingly handsome face had he smiled or even looked pleasant. But there had been no peace or repose in that bleak weathered face, and the slitted gray eyes had been shockingly cold, trusting no one and caring for no one.

It had been the face of a man who had somehow gone wrong and knew it but no longer cared. Not in the sense that he had become crooked or dishonest, but in the sense that he had become a killer, a man who did not value human life, including his own, and who did not hesitate to use his gun when provoked. A man who had no friends and wanted none, preferring to be around the sort of men who deserved his hard-eyed company, when he had to be around anyone.

Knell realized that he was on the verge of becoming like that himself. He had gotten so he felt more at ease around the sort of people whose opinions did not matter, when he had to be around anyone. It was a bad sign, he thought. A very bad sign.

Tom Graben was a man he could admire and one whose esteem he valued, yet he was not at ease around the man and it was obvious that the feeling was mutual. A loner like himself, Tom Graben preferred his own company, and he did not seem to know what Knell was after or to trust him. Well, there was no reason why the man should trust him, Knell reflected. After all, he had been riding with the men who were trying to kill Graben, had even joined in the chase himself. And Tom Graben would have to be a mind reader to guess why he had done so.

Knell glanced down the canyon, then suddenly hid his cigar. A rider was coming up the canyon, and presently Knell could see that the horse was carrying double. The long pale hair of Gibby Tate showed behind Mac Radner's shoulder.

Knell sighed, surprised at his disappointment. He knew that girl was no good, that she was wild and a little crazy and would never bring any man much besides misery and bad luck. But there was something about her, something that made a man aware of the loneliness and emptiness inside him.

They disappeared beyond the house, and a few moments later Knell heard a wild howl of grief and rage when Mac discovered his dead brother.

Chapter 16

In the cold gray dawn, Tom Graben sat with his back against the mesa wall near the mouth of the cave. He had not slept and his eyes were bloodshot and bitter. Even if he managed to come out of this fight alive, he knew he would never get over what they had done to Frank, to say nothing of what they had done to Tom himself. The bitterness would never entirely leave him, but would seep through his soul like a sickness and remain until the day he died.

He had taken Frank's body to a place where he did not think it would be disturbed again, at least not for a while. Not that it really mattered anymore, for nothing could ever erase from Tom's mind what they had already done to his brother. But seeing that they all paid for what they had done might ease the bitterness a little.

He lifted the gun from his lap, wiped away the dust and checked the loads. He thrust the gun in his waistband and checked the other one that he carried in his holster. The sun was trying to rise behind a reddish haze in the east, and would have already been visible had it not been for the dust blown up by the wind during the night. It was time to get started. Mac Radner was probably already on his trail, and the others would be before long.

His horses stood waiting, the buckskin half asleep, the blue roan reaching his head toward a few stunted brown blades of grass. He got into the saddle and headed out through the rocky hills, leaving a trail that could be followed, but not so easily that it would look suspi-

cious. The wind started blowing again shortly after sunrise, stirring
up more dust. The barren gray mountains were shrouded in haze,
and looked bleaker than ever through Graben's weary, slitted eyes.
It was going to be an unpleasant day, and the wind and dust would
make it harder to spot anyone following him.

Barney Kester was on guard at the broken window, as he had
somehow known he would be, despite the fact that his left arm was
in a makeshift sling and throbbed with a dull ache. The bone was
not broken, but he was afraid the wound would become infected, if it
wasn't already. He would probably lose that arm, he thought bitterly.
Yet he blamed Tobe Unger more than he blamed Graben. Tobe never
should have sent him up that ridge alone after Graben. But more and
more it seemed that the big man was determined to get him killed
one way or another.

Now Unger and Dub Astin sat at the plank table eating breakfast
while Barney tried to eat standing up with only one hand and watch
the rocky ridge at the same time. It was not fair, and somehow, if
it was ever possible, he meant to see Tobe pay for it. He would find
some way to get even.

Unger turned his shaggy head to glare at him through glittering
bloodshot eyes. "You see anything?"

The rough tone made the little man stiffen and grind his teeth
with anger and resentment. "No, I don't see nothin'."

"Take a look out the other way," Unger growled. "He might circle
around."

Barney sneered at that. "He would of done it already, if he was
goin' to. He wouldn't wait till it was light."

"How the hell do you know?" Unger snarled. "He might be waitin'
to start shootin' the minute somebody opens that door."

Barney had not thought of that, but he was not in the mood to
admit it. Instead he said, "Then somebody else can open the door. I
done took enough chances lately."

"We'll see about that," Unger said darkly. "If you've let him sneak
up on us, you're the one should open the door."

When Barney had circled the table and was peering cautiously
out the front window, Dub glanced up with sleepy red eyes and asked,
"See anything of Knell out there anywheres?"

"I don't see nobody."

"He prob'ly lit out last night," Unger said bitterly. "I knowed we couldn't count on him."

"I still say he's the man we saw at Turley's," Barney said. "I don't care what nobody else says."

"No, he ain't the one," Astin said. "I thought at first he was, but that was only because of his hair and them black clothes. That feller at Turley's had sort of pale gray or blue eyes, and Knell's eyes is nearly black."

"I still say it's him, I don't care what color his eyes is," Barney insisted. "And if he comes back I say we kill him, before he turns that gun on us."

"That's something else," Astin said. "That feller at Turley's had two Smith & Wesson pistols, and Knell's only got one Colt."

"That's all you've seen anyway," Barney sneered. "I'd sure like to see what's in them saddlebags."

A short time later, as they were mounting their gaunt, sleepy-eyed horses, Knell suddenly rode out of the rocks and walked his dark bay toward them.

"Bastard!" Barney Kester whispered, his good hand quivering near the butt of his holstered gun. But fear prevented the hand from actually touching the gun, for he knew that if he did touch the gun he would die. He knew it as surely as he was sitting his horse there in the hazy morning sunlight, watching the lean man in black ride toward them. Knell's dark eyes were on that hand and deliberately remained there until the hand moved away from the gun.

Tobe Unger had his big shaggy head cocked to one side, his bright narrow eyes glittering at Knell. "Where the hell you been?" he barked.

"Around," Knell said easily, as he reined in facing them. "You fellows ready to go?"

"I didn't think you'd come back," Unger said bluntly. "Not to he'p us anyway." His hard eyes darted briefly aside at Kester, and he added maliciously, "Barney's been sayin' you're Frank Graben, the man they saw at Turley's. What do you think of that?"

Knell's dark eyes shifted to the little man, and he said idly, "Maybe Barney believes in ghosts."

"Maybe I do!" Barney retorted. "I ain't the only one! A lot smarter folks than any of us swears there's ghosts! And I say you're either that man or his ghost! Maybe he took over your body somehow. I've heard of such things—"

"Shut up!" Tobe Unger yelled hoarsely. "He's got you spooked and you're talkin' crazy! When this is over I'll have to decide what to do about you, Barney. I can't have a man around me with the shakes, and you've got 'em bad."

"Is that why you been tryin' so hard to get me killed?" Barney asked.

"You'd be better off dead, the shape you're in," Unger said brutally.

Barney opened his mouth to protest, but thought better of it when he saw the threatening glitter in Tobe's eyes. The big man glared at him in silence for a moment, then reined his horse up the trail through the rocks, the others falling in behind. All of them watched the rocks with sharp, worried eyes, in case Graben was still around.

All except Mark Knell, who did not seem too concerned. He reined his horse alongside Kester's and looked at the little man with a hint of humor in his dark gray eyes. "I've been thinking about what you said back there, Barney. You know, you could be right. Lately I haven't seemed like myself at all. I've been doing all kinds of strange things I never did before."

The little man looked at him with wild eyes. Barney sensed that the tall dark stranger was playing some kind of game with him, deliberately picking on him the way everyone else did because of his size and because he was vulnerable and sensitive. But that in no way lessened Barney's conviction that there was something sinister and unnatural about Knell. This was just his way of toying with Barney and tormenting him.

Barney's voice was shrill as he said, "You keep away from me, you hear! I don't want you nowhere around me!" When Knell made no move to go away, Barney cried, "Tobe, you better keep him away from me!"

Unger was riding with the shotgun across his saddle. A moment before it had been in his mind to tell Knell to ride up front with him where he could keep an eye on him. But now he glanced around with open malice in his eyes and said, "No, you stick with him, Barney. You ain't no good for nothin' else, so I want you to keep a eye on him, just in case he is Frank Graben's ghost."

Barney Kester trembled with fear and frustration, but he knew it would be pointless to say anything more. Now they had all teamed up against him. He had never before felt so helpless, yet he could not recall a time when he had known such consuming bitterness, such an overwhelming desire to get even with the whole world.

How he longed to be a tough, dangerous man like Mark Knell, the very man he feared and hated!

As the crow flies Tom Graben was scarcely a mile away. He was still in the rough broken country between the old Tate shack and Radner Canyon. Everywhere a man rode in that area he was surrounded by buttes and rock formations and boulder-strewn ridges where nothing grew but a few stunted, twisted cedars and an occasional tuft of bleached dead grass. He was tired of being hemmed in and longed to be down on the flats where there was sage if nothing more. But this was a better place to make a stand, and he wanted to get this thing over with. He knew that before long they would be coming after him, but some of them would not go back.

He reined in among some huge boulders and glanced at the sky. It was covered with a dirty gray haze which all but hid the sun, but he did not know what it meant. He had been watching the weather all his life but he could still no more predict what it would do than he could predict what a woman would do. The gloom of twilight lingered, adding to the drab grayness of the landscape.

The shot, when it came, was completely unexpected. Someone—probably Mac Radner—must have got an early start and made better time on his trail than he had thought possible. But then he had not been in any hurry and evidently that had given someone a chance to overtake him.

The shot came from somewhere in the rocks behind him and the bullet whistled past his ear. He dived out of the saddle, rolled for cover and came to a stop behind a low rock with a gun in his hand, his gaunt stubbled face and cold blue eyes raised cautiously above the rock. But he saw nothing at which to shoot. Radner or whoever it was had timed his shot so that a gust of wind had blown the puff of smoke away and dissipated it.

It had been the crashing report of a rifle, not the bark of a hand-gun, and Graben knew he might soon be pinned down here—if he was not already.

Keeping low, he started to crawl out from behind the rock, then jumped back. Nothing happened, and after a few minutes he tried it again. This time he kept crawling until he was in a narrow opening between two tall rocks. Then he got to his feet and began picking his way carefully though the rocks in a crouch, his pale eyes searching in every direction.

He stopped behind a stunted cedar and looked up at a ridge of rocks and boulders. Yet in the cracks more cedars grew, twisted out of shape by the wind. The marksman could be somewhere along that ridge—or almost anywhere else, by now. One thing was all but certain—he would not still be where he had been when the shot was fired. Yet Graben, like a fool, was trying to close in on that abandoned spot, while the ambusher was no doubt looking for a new spot—or closing in on *him*.

The rifle worried him. That meant it was almost certainly Mac Radner, for none of Unger's men owned a rifle. In fact, Graben had not known that the Radners had one, though it seemed likely that men like them would have a long gun to shoot meat with, if for no other reason.

Then another thought suddenly occurred to him. Radner might find himself a spot where he could watch Graben's horses and wait for him to return to them. Then, without a word of warning, Radner would kill him.

With that thought in mind, Graben began making his way cautiously back toward the two horses. There was no way to figure out which spot Radner might pick to wait. There were too many suitable places for a dry-gulcher in the vicinity, all of them affording a view of the horses. What worried Graben now was the possibility that it might already be too late to get the horses out of sight in the rocks. The dry-gulcher might already have them in his sights, waiting for Graben to step into the saddle or grab the reins.

And Radner had plenty of time. Graben didn't. Unger and the others might have heard that shot and be on their way here even now. Graben did not want to fight them all at once, if he could help it.

He stopped in the narrow space between the two rocks where he could see the horses. They were as he had left them, the buckskin half asleep, the blue roan's head in the air, his bright dark eyes turned toward Graben.

Now if he could just get them to come to him. He was about to call softly to the horses when his eye caught a movement off to his left. A moment later, his gun ready, he saw the girl, Gibby Tate, slipping silently through the rocks toward the horses.

His first thought was that she might once again be trying to steal one of his animals, this time to make her escape on. But how did she happen to be here, in this particular place at this particular time? Graben thought about it while he watched her creep toward the horses, both of them now showing signs of nervousness at her approach.

The only answer he could come up with was that she must have come with Mac Radner and Mac must have sent her to get the horses, intending to put Graben afoot and then hunt him down like an Apache.

Graben waited until she had the reins of both horses in her hand, and then he raised his gun and said quietly, "Now bring them over here."

Startled, she looked at him and gasped. Then she threw a wild glance up at the rocks were Mac Radner must be waiting. She took a deep breath and said, "If I do, he'll kill me."

So Graben had been right. She had come with Radner. "If you don't, I will," he said. "Take your choice."

She hesitated, looking toward the rocks where Mac Radner waited, her face pale with fear, a wild look in her eyes. Then she came toward Graben—walking between the two horses. A smart girl, in her way.

Mac Radner's rifle crashed. The blue roan screamed and fell against the buckskin, almost crushing the girl between the two animals. But somehow she escaped uninjured and pulled the buckskin on toward the rocks while the dying roan lurched about crazily and then collapsed to the ground with the heavy pack.

With his left hand Graben jerked the buckskin's reins from the girl's hand, and then he put a bullet in the blue roan's brain to end the animal's terrible death struggles. He did it with a feeling of sadness and regret. He had wanted to keep that horse, not just because it was a fine animal, but most of all because it had belonged to Frank.

He pulled the buckskin to safety between the two rocks, and then he shoved the frightened girl back out into the open. "Get away from me," he said harshly. "You can take your chances with Radner."

She gave him a scared look and then ran back the way she had come. She was almost to the rocks on the other side when Radner's rifle roared again. She fell, but then rose and scrambled on into the rocks. Graben thought she had tripped on something a moment before the rifle crashed, but he could not be sure, and did not know whether she had been hit or not. He did not much care.

Then it occurred to him that, wounded or not, she might try to sneak back and get the horse she had ridden here. The same thought might also have occurred to Mac Radner, and he might start watching his own horses, for there was a chance that the girl might take both of them to prevent Mac from coming after her.

To Graben's left there was a hole between two rocks, blocked at the back end by another rock. Here he left the buckskin, and then he set off to find Mac Radner's horses. Two could play that game, he thought.

CHAPTER 17

Graben knew that the chance of finding the horses before the girl reached them was slight. But she was in almost as much danger now as Graben was, and she would have to move just as slowly and carefully, keeping out of sight behind the rocks. Mac Radner had already shot at her twice and might do so again.

Finding a path through the rocks was no trouble. There were natural paths winding away in every direction. But some afforded less cover than others. The one Graben chose was almost a tunnel in places, and there were only a few spots along the way where his skin contracted against the expectation of a bullet.

When he had gone about fifty yards he heard a shot and a scream not far ahead of him, followed by the pound of hoofs racing away. Evidently the girl had reached the horses and grabbed one of them, and Radner had fired at her. But whether she had been hit this time or merely frightened was only a guess.

Graben moved ahead cautiously and a moment later he peered around a low cedar stirring in the breeze and saw a fine looking sorrel standing in a little opening among the rocks. The horse was saddled, the reins tied to another cedar.

Graben heard rapid footsteps approaching and he crouched down behind the cedar, his gun cocked and ready. Moments later Mac Radner emerged from the rocks, his dark face contorted with anger, a look of silent rage in his black eyes. He went directly to the sorrel,

jerked the reins free and stepped into the saddle, apparently meaning to go after the girl. Preventing her escape seemed more important
to him at the moment than getting Graben.

He was reining the horse around, the single-shot rifle across the
saddle in front of him, when Graben rose to his feet and said sharply,
"Hold it!"

Radner jerked the rifle up to fire at him, but Graben fired first,
and the .44 slug lifted Radner out of the saddle.

The rifle clattered on the rocks. The horse, a well-trained animal,
stopped in its tracks the moment Radner's weight left the saddle.
Graben walked carefully around the horse and found Mac Radner
lying motionless on his side, his black eyes open in a blank stare.
Graben bent down and pulled the dead man's pistol from its holster,
ramming it into his own belt. He picked the old single-shot rifle up,
looked at it, then threw it away into the rocks.

Even as the rifle left his hand, he regretted the decision. For at
that very instant, someone fired a shot at him from near the crest
of the high rocky ridge. Out of the tail of his eye he saw the puff of
smoke and heard the bullet scream off a rock beside him, drawing a
nervous nicker from the sorrel. He threw a glance at the ridge and
saw Dub Astin dodge back out of sight.

Graben gave the sorrel a slap on the rump to send it away to safety, and he himself dived for cover as more lead streaked at him from
the ridge. He fired at a puff of smoke and heard an angry curse when
his bullet sprayed rock fragments in Tobe Unger's scowling face. Now
he knew where at least two of them were.

With a faint grim smile on his gaunt face, Graben took time to
reload. Then he checked the gun he had taken from Mac Radner. It
was an almost new Colt .45 with a long barrel and black hard-rubber
grips. Graben already had plenty of guns and ammunition, but most
of them were in his saddlebags on the buckskin and in the pack on
the dead roan. Realizing he might need the Peacemaker before this
was over, he crawled over to the dead man, unbuckled his shell belt
and pulled it free. He shoved the .45 in the holster and placed the belt
and holstered gun on the ground near him, deciding this might be as
good a place as any to make his stand.

Up on the ridge, Dub Astin crawled over to Tobe Unger and said, "I
shore wish I had that rifle he throwed away. What did he do that for?"

"How the hell should I know?" Unger grumbled, trying to wipe the dust and grit out of his red eyes. "Maybe he didn't figger he'd need it. That bastard can shoot!"

"He shore as hell can." Astin squatted behind a rock and thoughtfully rolled a smoke, squinting at the pale sun in the hazy sky. "I reckon that was Mac Radner's old gun, so he must of got Mac."

Unger glared at the lanky Texan in irritation and then said gruffly, "Guess so. If anybody's gonna get Graben, it will have to be us—you and me. We can't count on them other two for nothin'." He glanced about with glittering eyes. "Where did they get off to anyway?"

"I saw Knell snakin' down through the rocks and Barney taggin' after him like he was scared Knell might turn and bite him."

"He better keep a eye on that bastard, like I told him," Unger snarled. "I don't trust Knell no more than I do Graben."

Dub Astin nodded agreement. After smoking his cigarette in silence for a moment, he said, "I keep thinkin' about that rifle. I think I know about where it landed. If I could sneak down there and get it, then find me a good spot behind Graben—we'd have him between us. You get a little closer with that scattergun, and me with a rifle—it would be like a turkey shoot."

Unger gave him a hard, scornful glance. "Ain't you forgettin' one important little item? That gun prob'ly ain't even loaded. And you ain't got no shells for it."

"I'm purty shore it's loaded," Astin said calmly. "Mac never fired down there when Graben did, and I know Mac would of reloaded atter he fired that last time. And one good shot with that rifle is all I need."

Mark Knell was crawling silently through the rocks, taking his time. Barney Kester panted after him, wincing at the pain in his injured arm. When Knell stopped, Barney stopped. Knell peered down the slope for a moment, then he glanced around and saw the little man gripping his pistol in his hand, as if afraid to point it at him and pull the trigger.

There was a trace of bleak humor in Knell's dark eyes as he said, "You can't kill me, Barney. I'm already dead, remember?"

Barney shivered as if he had a chill, and lowered his gun. After a moment he asked, "What you up to?"

"What do you mean?" Knell asked with complete indifference, again glancing down the slope.

"I know you're up to something," Barney said. "But you better not try nothin', 'cause I'm watchin' you, just like Tobe said to."

Down at the foot of the slope, Graben added a sixth cartridge in each of the open-top Colts and slipped one of the guns back into the holster. His mouth was dry and he kept thinking about the canteen on his saddle. He wished he had brought the canteen with him, for he might be pinned down here for quite a while. He did not know how long this would last, for he intended to make them come after him.

He was pretty sure that Unger and Astin were already working their way down the rocky slope toward him. He had seen something moving around up there. He did not know where Knell and Barney Kester were, and that worried him. He still did not know what Knell might do when the chips were down, and that also worried him. It also annoyed him a little. He liked to know where people stood and what they were up to, so he could decide how to deal with them. He had never liked games, no matter who played them.

He peered cautiously up the slope, watching for movement, but the only movement he saw was the stunted cedars stirring in the wind. The sun rose higher and burned through the dirty gray haze.

He thought about the girl, Gibby Tate, and wondered if she had been hit. She was a mighty fine looking girl. Too bad she was so treacherous and so twisted inside. Not just twisted with hate, like a lot of men he had known. There was something else wrong with her. She was a little crazy, like her mother, and not worth all the trouble she would cause any man foolish enough to hook up with her. Mac Radner had found that out, but too late. She had got him killed.

Graben saw movement again on the slope, not far below the crest. Tobe Unger was scrambling from one rock to another lower down, hampered by his size and the shotgun he was carrying. Graben did not like the idea of letting the big man get in range with that scattergun, and he threw a quick shot that made Unger scramble faster for the shelter of the next rock. Then, in sheer rage, the big man fired both barrels down the slope. Graben could hear buckshot raining all around him even as the thunder of the shotgun shattered the air.

He ducked and shifted his position before raising his head again. But Unger was ready for him. Graben saw the big man scowling down the twin barrels of the shotgun at him, and he ducked again an instant before buckshot exploded from both muzzles.

Then, even before the buckshot quit falling around him, he bobbed up and fired, and was pleased to see his bullet jerk Unger's hat from his shaggy head. The big man's mouth fell open in alarm and he jerked his head down behind the rock.

During this time Dub Astin had not been idle. He had been crawling quickly and quietly down the slope while Graben's attention was on Tobe Unger. He found the single-shot rifle, made sure it was loaded, and then crawled on through the rocks, circling around behind Graben.

Mark Knell saw Astin slipping through the rocks behind Graben and a little above him. Astin found the spot he wanted behind a rock about waist high. He brought the rifle to his shoulder and rested his left elbow on the rock, squinting down the barrel at Graben.

He was already taking up the slack on the trigger when Knell fired. The rifle clattered to the ground. Astin stood straight up behind the rock with a look of dull wonder on his sunburnt face, then fell face down over the rock.

"You killed Dub!" Barney Kester screamed, leaping to his feet in his excitement. "Tobe, Knell has killed Astin!"

Unger bellowed like an enraged bull. "Kill the bastard!"

Graben had seen the little man standing there on the rocky slope, yelling excitedly. Without any hesitation but also without hurry, Graben turned his long-barreled .44 on the little man and squeezed the trigger.

Barney flinched as the bullet struck him. He gave Knell a bitter accusing look as if it were all his fault, and then fell forward on his face.

"Knell!" Unger shouted. "Is Barney dead?"

Knell glanced at the little man on the ground. "Afraid so."

"What did you kill Astin for?" Unger cried hoarsely. "Whose side are you on anyway?"

Knell did not bother to answer.

"Unger!" Graben called. "It's just you and me now! There's nobody left for you to send after me! You'll have to come yourself this time! How does it feel?"

It was Unger's turn for silence. His face was drawn and pale and there was a look of dread in his eyes. He stayed down behind his rock, his sweaty hands gripping the shotgun.

After about a minute he roared, "Knell!"

There was no answer.

"Knell! I'll give you five hundred dollars to kill the bastard!"

"I can't hear you," Knell said.

"A thousand!"

"Sorry."

Unger cussed him savagely and bitterly.

"You coming, Unger?" Graben called.

"I'll be down there in a minute, Graben!" Unger shouted hoarsely, wiping his sweaty palms on his trousers. "And you better hope and pray he gets me, Knell, 'cause if he don't I'll be after you!"

Knell did not answer. He did not appear to be too worried about it.

Tobe Unger suddenly drew a deep breath into his broad chest and rose to his feet, charging down the slope like a grizzly bear, making strange half-human noises, his scowling dark face contorted with fear and hatred. He had the shotgun at the ready and he fired both barrels the instant he saw Graben's face appear above the rock. The face disappeared and the big man kept running down the slope, breaking the shotgun open and fumbling in more shells.

His eyes were on the shotgun and he did not even see Graben this time when he looked over the rock and brought up his long-barreled revolver. Graben squeezed off his shot and the shotgun flew out of Unger's hands. He fell with a loud grunt and slid and rolled down the slope until a rock stopped him. Then he was still and silent and obviously dead. It was all over.

But Graben remained where he was, keeping out of sight behind his rock. For he was still not too sure about Mark Knell.

And Knell, realizing this, holstered his gun and got to his feet with a bleak look in his dark eyes. He turned and walked back up the rocky slope and over the crest of the ridge without looking again in Graben's direction.

The next day Knell rode up to Crazy Cora Tate's shack and found the blond-haired girl piling rocks on two fresh graves near the shack.

"Unger and who else?" he asked.

She glanced up at him in surprise. "Oh, I ain't goin' to bother about him," she said. "The buzzards are welcome to him if they want him. This here's my mama's grave. I decided to bring her down off that mesa on one of them outlaw horses I found."

"Who's in that one?"

"Oh, that's Frank Graben in that one. I had to throw a rope over a stout mesquite limb and loop it under his arms, with the other end tied to the horn of my saddle. Then I walked my horse off apiece and left him standin' there holdin' that dead man up high enough for me to get him on another horse. I managed to get him in the cave that night without any help. I'm a lot stronger than I look."

The girl was silent for a moment, looking at the two fresh graves with her strange pale eyes. "When I found that dead man layin' there beside my mama in that grave on the mesa, I was never so scared in all my life. Then I realized Tom Graben put him there on purpose to get even with me for diggin' his brother up. I started to hack that old corpse all to pieces. But then I got to thinkin'. In a way it seemed fittin' for them to be buried beside each other, so I brought him down too and buried him here beside her. I don't know if Tom Graben will like it or not, but he ain't come around and said nothin' about it." Then she asked, "You got any idea where he is?"

Knell shook his head. "No, but I sort of doubt if you'll ever see him again." He was thoughtful for a moment. "He reminds me a little of a man I knew once."

"What was his name?"

"He called himself Dan Potter, but I don't think that was his real name. I saw him again later on, in a different place, and he was calling himself Dan Prescott. I think that was his real name."

"Is Knell your real name?" the girl asked.

"Yes, it's my real name."

"That's a odd name for a man to have," she said. "How do you spell it? N-e-l-l?"

"K-n-e-l-l. Like in death knell."

"Then I reckon it fits you," she said.

Mark Knell thought about it for a moment, his dark eyes somber. Then he said, "Yes, I reckon it does."

What are you goin' to do now?" Gibby Tate asked.

"Ride on, I guess. No reason to stay now."

"There's no reason for me to stay either," the girl said. "I was thinkin' maybe I could ride along with you a piece."

A shadow seemed to settle over Mark Knell's lean dark face. "I don't think that would be a good idea," he said.

"Why not?" she asked in surprised.

"I always ride alone," he said.

"Why's that?"

"I don't know," he said. "It's just the way I am."

About this time, on the outskirts of Rock Crossing, Tom Graben met a rider headed for the Hopkins ranch. The two men drew rein, passed the time of day and smoked a cigarette.

As he was about to ride on, Tom Graben looked off toward the bleak gray mountains beyond the town and said quietly, "Tell her I'm all right." After a moment he added, "Tell her maybe I'll come back someday."

Thank you for reading
The Revenge of Tom Graben
by Van Holt.

We hope you enjoyed this story. If so, please leave a review about
your experience so others may discover Van Holt.

You may also enjoy another story about some famous gunfighters
called *Maben*

Excerpt from
MABEN
By Van Holt

The man who called himself John Parker rode into Live Oaks shortly after
noon and tied his black horse in front of the Alamo Saloon, glancing briefly
along the short crooked street that ran between the log shacks and flat-
roofed adobes. He pulled his black hat a little lower over his gray eyes and
stepped in through the swing doors and stopped at the front end of the plank
bar.

A red-faced, heavyset man standing farther down the bar bared
his big teeth in a smile and looked the dark-garbed stranger over
with frank curiosity. His eyes lingered on the wide shell belt and
walnut-butted Colt pistols in the tied-down holsters. There was no
one else in the saloon except the bartender, who set out a bottle and
glass when the stranger asked for whiskey.

While Parker sipped his drink in silence, the heavyset man continued to study his somber gray eyes and bleak weathered face. At
last he chuckled and said, as though making a joke, "Who was it died,
stranger? Somebody close to you?"

Parker's gray eyes narrowed to glittering slits. "About as close as
you're standing," he said quietly.

The stout man quit grinning and his face got a little redder.

Parker turned to the bartender. "Can you tell me where I can find
an old man named Maben? I understand he lives around here."

The bartender looked uncomfortable and glanced at the stout
man, who said, "What did you want to see him about, stranger?"

"I owe him some money."

The stout man laughed. "That's one debt you won't never have to pay, stranger. Old man Maben was found dead at his shack about a week ago."

There was no change on Parker's lean brown face. But he was silent and motionless for so long that the bartender and the red-faced man began to fidget nervously. At last he asked, "How did he die?"

The stout man shrugged. "Somebody shot him. Injuns, like as not. We're always havin' trouble with them red devils around here. Mostly Comanches, but sometimes it's Apaches raidin' over this way from New Mexico and Arizona. He wasn't scalped nor hacked up, so it was prob'ly Apaches. They don't go in for that like them Comanches do."

There was something skeptical, doubting in Parker's silence, in the very blankness of his long hard face, as though he was not quite buying the fat man's story. But when he spoke his tone was quiet and indifferent. "How do I find his place? I guess the least I can do is ride by there."

"It's in the brush about five miles down the valley. You'll know it by the fresh grave. But if I was you I'd make it a short visit. Old Maben just built that old shack on open range, and now that he's dead there's others around here figgerin' to use that land."

"That wouldn't have anything to do with his death, would it?" Parker asked dryly.

The red-faced man looked startled. "Not as far as I know. It sure wasn't none of my boys. I can't speak for nobody else. There's some around here that would do almost anything."

Parker did not appear to be listening. He laid some silver on the bar and strolled outside. The street and the scattered houses were shaded by live oaks and cottonwoods. Even on hot days it should be nice and cool here. This was late fall and there was a bite in the air.

Parker walked past the general store, in front of which stood a buckboard loaded with supplies. On the seat sat two very pretty girls still in their teens. One had yellow hair and blue eyes, the other red hair and dark eyes.

A smiling handsome young man on a sorrel horse had reined in beside the buckboard to talk to them. Now he turned his reckless blue eyes toward Parker.

"Better watch out," the redheaded girl said in a low voice, noticing Parker's guns and his cold eyes. "He's a killer."

She was smiling as she said it and her lovely red mouth was twisted with mild scorn. Her indifference to Parker was obvious. She had seen two-gun strangers before. They were not uncommon in southwest Texas in the 1870's.

Parker gave her a cool glance and went on by, turning into the restaurant next door to the store. Behind him he heard the young man say, "You could be right. He may be a killer."

While Parker was eating warmed-over steak and potatoes in the restaurant, several riders cantered into town, pulling up before the Alamo Saloon. A few minutes later all five of them tramped into the restaurant and stood glaring at him through mean, hard eyes. They were bearded, ragged, dirty. All wore guns and looked ready to use them.

The apparent leader of the bunch, a big tough-looking man in his thirties, grated, "Hear you been askin' about old man Maben. What's he to you?"

Parker raised his eyes briefly from his food. He had cut the tough steak into small pieces and was now carelessly eating with the fork in his right hand. His left was out of sight under the table. "Was, you mean," he said.

The big man silently nodded, watching him.

"What's it to you?" Parker asked.

"I'm askin' the questions," the big man said nastily. "You better speak up, if you know what's good for you."

"And if I don't?" Parker asked.

"Then I reckon we'll have to beat it out of you."

Parker saw the waitress, a thin pale girl, watching him with worried eyes.

Under the table, his left hand eased a long-barreled revolver from its holster and lifted it above the table. The big man's eyes widened as Parker's thumb cocked the hammer.

One of the other men went for his gun and Parker shot him in the arm, as though casually shooting at a target.

"Anybody else?" Parker asked, watching them through his cold gray eyes.

No one moved or spoke.

Parker deliberately finished his coffee, keeping them covered with the long-barreled .44 in his left hand. Then he got up from the table and said, "Outside. Move."

They moved outside and he followed them. He marched them to a huge old oak at the edge of the street and then said to the big man, "I guess you're pretty handy with your fists, especially when you've got four men to help you."

The big man glared back at him and said nothing.

"You wanted to fight," Parker said. "Let's see you fight that tree. Go on, hit it."

The big man blinked in surprise.

Parker cocked his gun. "I said hit it."

The big man took a deep breath, then hit the oak trunk with his fist.

"Harder!"

The big man hit the tree again, then bent over holding his smashed hand and groaning.

"Any of you other boys like to use your fists?" Parker asked.

None of them said anything, but the man with the bleeding arm shook his head miserably.

Parker heard a horse walking behind him and shot a quick glance over his shoulder. The handsome young man reined in and chuckled at the men standing under the live oak.

"You boys having fun?" he asked.

The big man cussed. "Keep ridin', Billy. We'll get around to you later."

Billy folded both hands on the saddle horn and yawned. "That ain't no way to talk, Dave. I thought we were friends."

"Friends, hell! If you don't leave my girl and my cows alone, I'll make you wish you'd never got born!"

Billy laughed. "You're dreaming, Dave. Molly told me she wouldn't get near you if you were the only man in Texas. And them cows belong to whoever can catch them."

"Like hell! Not when they're on my range! You keep the hell off!"

"You can't have it all, Dave. You'll have to leave a little for the rest of us."

"I'll kill any man tries to take what's mine!"

"It don't look to me like you're in no shape to back up that kind of talk, Dave," Billy said, casually rolling a cigarette. "What happened to your hand?"

"Never you mind! And keep off the Maben place. I'm takin' it over. He was squattin' on my range anyway."

Billy was still smiling as he said, "That why you killed him?"

"It was you, more likely!" Dave retorted.

"You know me better than that, Dave."

"The hell I do! You'd shoot your own mother just to see her kick!"

"You're getting yourself all mixed up, Dave. The way I heard it, it was you who shot your mother, and your pa too. And everybody around here knows I liked old man Maben. You're the one who kept trying to run him off."

"He was on my range, like I said."

"How you figger that, Dave? He was here first."

"Look who's talkin'! You rode in a few months ago and started actin' like the whole country belongs to you!"

"It's all open range, Dave. It belongs to everybody."

"That ain't the way it works around here! A man takes what he needs and holds it if he's man enough! I'm plenty man enough, as you'll find out!"

Dave turned his wild eyes on Parker. "That goes for you too! You were lucky enough to get the drop on us this time, with that sneaky trick you pulled. But the next time we'll be holdin' the guns. If you're smart you'll start ridin' and not let us catch you."

"I think I'll stay a while," Parker said. "I'll be at the Maben place, when you feel lucky."

"It looks like there'll be another grave there before long," Dave said. "That's the only way you'll stay at the Maben place!"

With that he turned his broad back and tramped toward the Alamo Saloon. The other four tramped after him. The chunky fellow stood before the saloon grinning at the spectacle they made. Dave knocked him down, then grabbed his injured hand and howled.

The young man on the sorrel laughed and turned his bright blue eyes to Parker. "That's Dave Shiner and his boys," he said. "You better watch out for them."

Parker eased the hammer down on his gun and slipped it back into the holster. "They better watch out for me," he said.

"You left-handed?" Billy asked curiously.

"I'm left-handed and right-handed."

"So am I," Billy said. He was also wearing two guns, but his had ivory handles. "I'm Billy Brink."

"John Parker."

Billy Brink smiled. "I had a feeling you might be Frank Maben, old man Maben's long lost son. He told me he had a boy he hadn't seen since before the war."

Parker scowled. "What else did he tell you?"

"Not too much. Said he came out here in '63 from Virginia, because he didn't want no part of the war. Said his wife was dead and maybe his son didn't know where he was, if he wasn't killed in the war."

"Maybe he was killed in the war," Parker suggested.

Billy Brink shrugged and flipped his cigarette over the sorrel's head. "Well, I'll mosey along. I promised to catch up with them Baber girls and make sure they get home all right. They shouldn't of come off by theirselves, but their pa and brothers took a herd to Wichita and ain't got back yet."

"They sisters?" Parker asked.

"Cousins. Helen's folks are dead."

"Which one's she?"

"The redhead." Billy grinned. "You can have her. She's too wild even for me."

"I figured that blonde might be pretty wild."

"They're both wild as mustangs. Takes a man to ride them."

Parker changed the subject. "Any idea who killed the old man?"

Billy Brink drew a deep breath. "I couldn't say. But it wasn't Indians. He had some flour and stuff that they would have taken, or scattered all to hell. I've seen places where they raided."

"What about his stock?"

"All he had was a few horses. He told me he sold all his cattle a couple years back. Before that he branded wild cattle out of the brush, like everybody else around here. He had several hands and sold a herd or two every year. Everybody thinks he had money hid around there somewhere, and nearly everybody around here's been out there to look for it. But I don't think they had any luck."

"There any law around here?" Parker asked.

"Every man packs his own in his holster."

"That's what I figured," Parker said. "By the way, who buried the old man?"

"I did." Billy Brink touched his hat and started off on the sorrel. "I'll see you around."

Parker watched him go, then walked back to the saloon to get his horse. Dave Shiner and his men were still inside. The red-faced man stood in front of the saloon rubbing his jaw.

"You lookin' for a job?" he asked Parker.

"Depends on who's hiring."

"I am. Beef Tuggle. I need a man who can handle Dave Shiner and his boys. My men are scared of them."

"Afraid you'll have to do your own fighting," Parker said. "You couldn't afford me."

"What makes you say that?"

"Take my word for it."

Parker untied his black gelding and stepped into the saddle, glancing at the brand on the Shiner horses.

"If you change your mind, ride over to see me," Tuggle said. "Anybody can tell you how to find the Lazy T."

Parker studied him from the saddle. "How many horses did Maben have?"

"Not many. But they were the best in the country." Tuggle grinned. "I guess that's why the Injuns and white horse thieves picked on him. There might still be four or five around there, but you won't find many."

"What brand did he use?" Parker asked.

"The Rockin' Chair. I guess he picked that brand 'cause he was so fond of his rockin' chair. Used to sit out on his porch with his pipe and rock and smoke half the time, after he went out of the cattle business. I think he was sittin' out there when he was shot."

To continue reading MABEN,

Click or go here:

Amazon: http://amzn.to/1judfzK

Barnes & Nobel: http://bit.ly/1eVnT22

CreateSpace: http://bit.ly/IvZvsF

Excerpt from
Rebel With A Gun
by Van Holt

On a gray, drizzly day in the spring of 1865, a tall slender young man on a brown horse rode along the muddy street of Hayville, Missouri. Several heads turned to stare at him, but he seemed not to notice anyone, and he did not stop in the town, but rode on out to a weather-beaten, deserted-looking house and dismounted in the weed-grown yard.

At the edge of the yard there was a grave surrounded by a low picket fence and he went that way and stood with his head bared in the slow drizzle and stared at the grave with bleak, bitter blue eyes. He was only nineteen but looked thirty. He had been only fifteen when the war started. That seemed like a lifetime ago, another world —a world that had been destroyed. All that was left was a deserted battlefield, a devastated wasteland swarming with scavengers and pillagers.

An old black man with only one eye appeared from a dripping pine thicket and slowly reached up to remove a battered hat and scratch the white fuzz on his head.

"Dat you, Mistuh Ben?"

"It's me, Mose," Ben Tatum said.

"I knowed sooner or later you'd come back to see yo' ma's grave. She died two years back now. Never was the same aftuh we heard the news about yo' pa. And too she was worried sick about you. Is it true you rode with Quantrill, Mistuh Ben?"

"You can hear anything, Mose."

"Yessuh, dat's de truth, it sho' is. But I wouldn't rightly blame you if you did. Dem Yankees sho' did raise hell, didn't they, Mistuh Ben?"

Old Mose was something of a diplomat. Had he been talking to a Yankee, he would have said it was the Rebels who had raised hell.

Or he might have said it was Quantrill's raiders.

"The war's over, Mose."

"Yessuh, I sho' do hope so, I sho' do." Old Mose reached up and rubbed his good eye, and for a moment his blind eye seemed to peer at the tall young man in the old coat. "But folks say there's some who still ain't surrendered and don't plan to. I hear there ain't no amnesty for Quantrill's men. Is dat true, Mistuh Ben?"

"That's what I heard, Mose."

"Dat sho' is too bad. I guess dat mean there still be ridin' and shootin' and burnin' just like befo'."

"Maybe not, Mose."

"I sho' do hope not. Has you only got one gun, Mistuh Ben? I hear some of Quantrill's men carry fo' or five all at one time."

Ben Tatum glanced down at the double-action Cooper Navy revolver in his waistband. He buttoned his coat over the gun. "I just got in the habit of carrying this one, Mose. I wouldn't feel right without it."

"Guess a man can't be too careful dese days." Old Mose thoughtfully rubbed the wide bridge of his nose, his good eye wandering off down the road toward Hayville. "Well, I just come by to check on yo' ma's grave. She sho' was a fine woman. Mistuh Snyder down to de bank own de place now. I guess you heard his boy Cal done gone and married dat Farmer girl you was sweet on?"

Ben Tatum let out a long sigh. "No, I hadn't heard, Mose. But it doesn't matter now. I can't stay here."

Old Mose looked like he had lost his only friend. "Where will you go, Mistuh Ben?"

"I don't know yet. West, maybe."

He turned and looked at the old house with its warped shingles and staring, broken windows. He did not go inside. He knew the house would be as empty as he felt.

He turned toward his horse.

"Oh, Mistuh Ben!"

"What is it, Mose?"

"I almost forgot," old Mose said, limping forward. "Yo' ma's sister, what live over to Alder Creek, she said if I ever saw you again to be sho' and tell you to come by and see her."

"All right, Mose. Thanks."

He thoughtfully reached into a pocket, found a coin and tossed it to the old Negro.

A gnarled black hand shot up and plucked the coin out of the air. "Thanks, Mistuh Ben. I sho' do 'preciate it. Times sho' is hard since they went and freed us darkies. Them Yankees freed us but they don't feed us."

He rode back through Hayville. The small town seemed all but deserted. But it had always seemed deserted on rainy days, and sometimes even on sunny days. But for some reason Ben Tatum could no longer recall very many sunny days. They had faded into the mist of time, the dark horror of war.

He stopped at a store to get a few supplies. The sad-eyed old man behind the counter seemed not to recognize him. But Ben Tatum had been only a boy when he had left, and now he was a tall young man with shaggy brown hair and a short beard. He had not shaved on purpose because he had no wish to be recognized. And he suspected that old man Hill did not recognize him on purpose. It was usually best not to recognize men who had ridden with Quantrill.

The slow rain had stopped, and when he left the store Ben Tatum saw a few people stirring about. A handsome, well-dressed young couple were going along the opposite walk. The young man had wavy dark hair and long sideburns, a neatly trimmed mustache. He wore a dark suit and carried a cane, like a dandy, and his arrogant face was familiar. The girl had long dark hair and just a hint of freckles. It was Jane Farmer. Only it would be Jane Snyder now. Cal Snyder had stayed here and courted her and married her while Ben Tatum was dodging bullets and sleeping out in the wet and cold, when he got a chance to sleep at all. Cal Snyder had not gone to the war. His father had hired a man to go in his place, a man who had not come back. He had been killed at Shiloh.

Ben Tatum stopped and stared at her as if a mule had kicked him in the belly. But neither Jane Snyder nor her dandified husband showed the slightest sign that they recognized him or even saw him. They went on along the walk and turned into the restaurant.

With a sick hollow feeling inside him, Ben Tatum got back in his wet saddle and rode on along the muddy street, returning to the bleak empty world from which he had come, homeless now and a wanderer forever. The war had taught him how to lose. Turn your back and ride off as if it did not matter. Never let the winners know you cared.

"Ben! Ben Tatum!"

For a fleeting moment hope rose up in him like an old dream returning. But then he realized that it was not her voice, and when he looked around he saw a fresh-faced girl just blooming into womanhood, a girl with long light brown hair that was almost yellow and a face that looked somehow familiar. She was smiling and radiant and seemed happy to see him. Puzzled, he searched his memory but failed to place her, and it made him uneasy. He lived in a world where it did not pay to trust your closest friends, much less strange beautiful girls who seemed too happy to see you. Many girls that age had been spies during the war and had lured many a dazzled man to their destruction. Some of them might still be luring men to their destruction, for the war still was not over for some men and never would be over. Men like Ben Tatum. And the fact that she knew his name proved nothing.

So he merely touched his hat and kept his horse at the same weary trot along the muddy street, and behind him he heard a little exclamation: "Well!" He rode on out of town, wondering who she was. He noticed that it had started raining again.

Alder Creek was a two-day ride west of Hayville. There were no streets in Alder Creek, just narrow roads that wound among the trees that grew everywhere, and most of the houses were scattered about in clearings that had been hacked out of the trees and brush.

Ben Tatum's aunt lived in a big old house on a shelf above the hidden murmuring creek that had given the town its name. Her husband had died years ago in a mysterious hunting accident and she had soon remarried and had a lively stepdaughter. Her two sons had died in the war and she had no other children of her own.

Cora Wilburn had been a slender, attractive woman in her late thirties the last time Ben Tatum had seen her. But the war had aged her as it had aged everyone else. There were lines in her tired face and streaks of gray in her hair, and she had put on weight. But she seemed glad to see him, and it was good to see a smiling, friendly face.

She hugged him and patted his back just the way his own mother would have done had she lived to see him come home. "My, you've sure grown into a tall, fine-looking man," she said, blinking away tears. Her voice sounded as old and tired as she looked. "But you need a haircut and some decent clothes. Sam's a pretty good barber, they tell me, and you can have some of Dave's clothes. He was tall like you. I appreciate the nice letter you sent me when Dave and Lot were killed."

He nodded, and just then he noticed a tall slender girl of about thirteen standing on the porch watching him with lively green eyes and a mischievous smile. "This can't be Kittie," he said in a slow surprise.

"Yes, that's Kittie," Cora Wilburn said in her tired voice. "Ain't she run up like a weed? Soon be grown. It's getting hard to keep the boys away from her or her away from the boys."

Kittie Wilburn gave her dark head a little toss and flashed her white teeth in a smile, but said nothing.

"Sam's at the barbershop," Cora Wilburn added. "Soon as you eat a bite and catch your breath, you should go on down there and get some of that hair cut off your head and face. I want to see what you look like without that beard."

Sam Wilburn was a strange, moody man, by turns silent and talkative. He had a habit of watching you out of the corners of cold green eyes, without ever facing you directly. He was trimming an old man's white hair when Ben Tatum opened the door of the small barbershop. He glanced up at him out of those strange green eyes and said, "Have a seat. I'll be with you in a few minutes."

Ben Tatum sat down in a chair against the wall and picked up an old newspaper. The war was still going on when the newspaper was printed, but Quantrill had already disappeared and was thought dead by them and his followers had scattered, some of them forming small guerrilla bands of their own, or degenerating into common outlaws and looters, preying on the

South as well as the North. Others had gone into hiding or left the country. Few had any homes left to return to, even if it had been safe to go home.

When the old man left, Ben Tatum took his place in the barber's chair and Sam Wilburn went to work on his hair. He did not seem very happy to see the younger man. They had never had much use for each other, and now and then Ben Tatum had idly wondered if Sam Wilburn had arranged the hunting accident that had left Cora Medlow an attractive young widow. Why Cora had married Sam Wilburn was another mystery he still had not figured out. But the world was full of things he would probably never understand.

Sam Wilburn glanced through the window at a wagon creaking down the crooked, stump-dotted road that passed for the town's main street. "I've been wondering when you'd show up," he said. When Ben Tatum made no reply, he asked, "You been to the house?"

Ben Tatum grunted in the affirmative.

Sam Wilburn worked in silence for a time, evidently doing a thorough job of it. The coarse brown hair fell on the apron in chunk's. Scattered among the brown, there were hairs that looked like copper wires, and there were more of them in his beard, especially on his chin. Those dark reddish copper hairs gleamed in his hair and short beard.

"What do you plan to do, now that the war's over?" Wilburn asked, his attention on his work.

"I ain't decided yet."

"You can't stay around here. They'll be looking for you."

Ben Tatum sighed, but said nothing. He sighed because he knew Sam Wilburn did not want him to stay around here. He had known already that they would be looking for him.

"Texas," Sam Wilburn said. "That's your best bet. I've been thinking about going down there myself. I don't think I'll like it much around here when the carpetbaggers move in. I don't like nobody telling me what to do or how to run my business."

"I doubt if it will be much better in Texas."

"Can't be any worse. Quite a few others around here and Hayville feel the same way. They've been talking about getting up a whole wagon train and going down there."

"I imagine talk about it is about all they'll ever do."

"No, they're serious. Even old Gip Snyder is talking about going. He says it's a new country with a lot of opportunities and we can build ourselves a new town down there where nobody won't bother us. Course, he plans to start a new bank, and I could start a new barbershop. The more I think about it, the better I like the idea."

"There'll be carpetbaggers in Texas just like there are here," Ben Tatum said.

"It won't be as bad. This state's been torn apart worse by the war than any other state in the country, and now that it's safe the carpetbaggers will be flocking in like vultures to pick our bones. Our money's already worthless. That's why old Gip Snyder is so keen on going. His bank at Hayville is in trouble, and he wants to salvage what he can and get out."

Ben Tatum shifted uncomfortably in the chair. "What about all the property he owns around Hayville?"

"I think he's found a buyer for most of it. That's the only thing that worries me. I don't know what I'd do with our property here if I went, and Cora ain't too keen on going. She's been in bad health lately. Losing them boys nearly killed her."

Ben Tatum was silent.

After a moment Wilburn asked, "What about the beard?"

"Get rid of it, I guess. Aunt Cora don't seem to like it."

After supper Ben Tatum went for a walk down along the creek. A path led him past an old shack almost hidden in the trees and brush. There was a light burning in the shack and through the window he caught a glimpse of a very shapely, blond-haired woman taking a bath. The long hair looked familiar.

When he got back to the Wilburn house he found Kittie in his room. "What are you doing here?" he asked, taking off the coat Aunt Cora had given him. It had belonged to Dave Medlow but it fitted Ben Tatum all right.

Kittie's lips curled back from her white teeth in a teasing smile. "Straightening up your room, Cousin Ben," she said with a deliberately exaggerated southern drawl.

"You run along," he said. "I'm not your cousin and the room don't need straightening up."

"That's right, we ain't cousins, are we?" she said. "We ain't no kin a'tall, now I think about it. But I was gonna marry you anyway. You sure do look handsome without that old beard. It made you look like a old man of about thirty."

"I'll be thirty before you're dry behind the ears," he said. He hung the coat in the closet and put his gun in a bureau drawer. In the mirror he saw Kittie Wilburn watching him with a smile, and he turned around with a frown. "Are you still here?"

"No, I'm still leaving. I just ain't got very far yet." She lay down on the bed and put her bare feet up on the gray wallpaper, so that her skirt fell down around her thighs, revealing very shapely legs for a skinny, thirteen-year-old girl. "Did you go see Rose?" she asked.

"Who?"

"Rose Harper. That girl who lives down by the creek. She just got back from Hayville a little while ago. I saw her go by. She lives over here now. Ever since she married Joe Harper. But she don't stay here much, 'cause he ain't never around. The bluebellies and nearly everybody else is looking for him, 'cause he rode with Quantrill. Like you."

"What does she look like?"

"Don't you know? You went to see her, didn't you? Anyway, you used to know her when she lived at Hayville with her folks."

"Wait a minute," Ben Tatum said. "Didn't Joe Harper marry that Hickey girl? Rose Hickey?"

"He shore did, Cousin Ben. He shore did."

"I thought that was what he told me after he came home the last time. My God, she was just a kid the last time I saw her."

"She ain't no kid now."

"She sure ain't," Ben Tatum agreed. "I saw her in Hayville and didn't even recognize her."

"I hate her," Kittie Wilburn said. "She makes me look plumb scrawny." She pulled her skirt up a little higher and looked at her thighs. "Do you think I'll ever outgrow it, Cousin Ben? Looking so scrawny and all?"

"You might," he said, "if I don't get mad and wring your neck."

"Oh, all right. I'll go." She swung her bare feet to the floor and rose, stretching and making a sort of groaning sound in her throat. She looked at him with that teasing smile. "But you've got to promise me something first."

"What?"

"I'll have to whisper it. I don't want anyone else to hear." She put her arms around his neck and rose on tiptoes, putting her warm moist lips close to his ear and whispering, "You've got to promise to marry me someday. Then I'll go."

"That'll be the day!"

She giggled and again made as if to whisper something, but this time she bit his ear and then ran from the room. At the door she pulled her skirt up to her waist, bent over and showed him her bottom. And it was quite a bottom for a skinny, thirteen-year-old girl to be flashing. He saw it in his mind until he went to sleep, and he wondered if he was the only one who had seen it. If so, it was probably only because she had not had an opportunity to show it to anyone else.

He knew he should tell Aunt Cora about the girl's naughty behavior, for her own good. But he also knew that he wouldn't, for his own good. Aunt

Cora might think he had encouraged the child in some way, and think less of him because of it.

He slept late the next morning, and was awakened by the slamming of the door when Sam Wilburn left for the barbershop. He had just gotten dressed when he heard a dozen or more horsemen crowding into the yard, ordering all those inside to come out with their hands in the air.

The preceding was from the western novel
Rebel With A Gun

To keep reading, click or go here:
http://amzn.to/1apARDN

Excerpt from
Dead Man Riding
by Van Holt

Nine tough-looking men, most of them bearded and dirty, all heavily armed, were lined up at the plank bar that windy Saturday afternoon when the stranger rode into the small adobe town of Bandanna. They heard the sound of his horse walking quietly down the short dusty street and then the creak of leather as he dismounted in front of the saloon.

Sharp eyes turned or watched him in the back-bar window as he came in through the batwing doors. They saw a tall young man in his late twenties, with broad shoulders and a lean waist. His hair was brown and thick under the wide-brimmed, low-crowned hat; his eyes were gray and cold under frowning brows. His coat was unbuttoned and they saw that he wore two guns, one in a tied-down holster, the other thrust into his waistband with the walnut butt to the right for a cross draw.

A noticeable change came over the nine men already at the bar. They exchanged silent glances, or stared hard at the tall stranger. Dark eyes got darker, pale eyes seemed to freeze in their sockets.

He stopped at the front end of the bar, several feet from Dudley Haskett, and said one quiet word to the chunky bartender.

"Whiskey."

The bartender put a bottle and a glass on the plank bar and then went back to polishing glasses. The saloon was so quiet that the noise made by the stranger uncorking the bottle seemed loud in the silence. Outside the wind moaned like a lost soul in limbo, but there was no other sound.

Then, as the stranger slowly sipped his whiskey, Haskett's dark beard parted in a white-toothed grin and he said, "You lookin' for work, stranger?"

The stranger glanced at him in surprise. The other men at the bar seemed equally surprised.

"Hadn't thought about it."

"I'm Dudley Haskett, foreman of the Spradlin ranch. You must of heard of Hoot Spradlin?"

"Can't say as I have."

Haskett's grin faded, to be replaced by a look of astonishment. "Then you must not be from these parts."

"Nope."

Haskett hesitated. "Mind if I ask yore name?"

"Frank Stanton."

There was a little intake of breath along the bar, a sudden tensing of gun hands.

Dudley Haskett leaned slightly toward him. "You mind sayin' that again?"

The stranger, still holding the glass in his left hand, repeated the name in the same quiet tone.

Haskett relaxed a little and his grin returned, but he continued to study the stranger closely. "There for a minute I thought you said Fanton. You wouldn't happen to know a man by that name, would you?"

"Fanton?" The stranger seemed to think for a moment, then shook his head. "No, I don't think so."

Haskett wiped his palms on his trousers, his eyes haunted. "Well, we were about to head back for the ranch. Be supper time 'fore we get there, and there don't seem to be much doin' in town. If you want to ride along, I'll speak to the boss about givin' you a job. But you might get stuck in a shack by yoreself or with just one other man, ridin' line. Ain't much else to do in the winter."

Stanton finished his drink. "I don't mind riding line."

Haskett's grin was uneasy. "Somehow I didn't figger you would."

They left money on the plank bar and filed outside. The hard-eyed Spradlin men watched Stanton mount his roan gelding. Then they silently untied their own horses and mounted up. Haskett and Stanton took the lead as they rode away from the bleak huddle of earth-colored buildings that was usually just called town. It was hardly ever called Bandanna.

Stanton glanced back once, then turned his gray eyes to the brush-spotted plains ahead. "The Spradlin ranch a pretty big outfit?" he asked as if just making idle conversation.

Haskett grinned. "One of the biggest in southwest Texas." Then he added, "We're on it now, as a matter of fact. Ain't no other ranches around but a few squatters that Hoot has been talkin' about runnin' off."

Stanton fell silent, his eyes strangely bleak and bitter under his wide hatbrim.

The ranch headquarters turned out to be a half-dugout sticking out of the side of a barren rocky hill dotted with dwarf cedars, a low adobe bunkhouse and cookshack adjoining, some sheds and a tangle of pole corrals. There was a spring nearby and a lonely old cottonwood tree whose bare branches rattled in the cold wind.

It was almost dark when the ten men arrived, but Stanton saw the rope dangling from the lowest limb of the cottonwood. There was an empty noose at the end of the rope and the rope swung in the wind.

"That's where we hung Fanton," Haskett said, watching him closely as they rode by the tree.

For a moment Stanton's hand went to his neck, but he said nothing.

The bunkhouse was dark, but lamplight showed at the cookshack and the half-dugout. The ten men dismounted at the corrals, and Haskett said, "One of you boys take care of Stanton's horse. Me and him will go in to see Hoot about that job."

Haskett and the tall silent stranger crossed to the half-dugout and passed in under a brush-roofed unfloored porch to enter a large long room that contained a combination bar and store counter at the front and living quarters at the back.

Two slender, attractive blond-haired women, one in her late thirties, the other a girl of about nineteen, were quietly eating supper at a plank table in the back. The girl, very pretty despite a pouting mouth and unhappy eyes, looked at Stanton with no hint of a smile. The older woman did not even glance in his direction, though she sat facing the door.

Behind the counter stood a lean dark man of about fifty. His eyes were black and malevolent, one much smaller than the other.

Haskett touched his hat to the two women at the back and then spoke to the dark man. "Got a man here lookin' for work, Hoot." There was a little pause before he added, "Says his name's Frank Stanton."

Hoot Spradlin's bigger eye widened in surprise, the other became a gleaming black slit. For a long moment he peered at Stanton in the dim lamplight, and what he saw did not lessen the suspicion and hatred in his eyes.

"Might be you wouldn't like it here," he said finally. "We have a lot of trouble with Comanches and white rustlers, not to mention greasers from across the border. We just buried two men. That's the only reason I'd be interested in hirin' you."

Stanton shrugged his broad shoulders. "That's about what I expected."

Hoot Spradlin stared at him a moment in silence, then reluctantly nodded. "Go to the bunkhouse and find yourself a bunk. And you better get on over to the cookshack or there won't be nothin' left."

Stanton silently nodded and turned to leave.

"You stay here a minute, Dudley," Spradlin said. "Somethin' I want to ask you."

Stanton paused outside in the gathering darkness and looked toward the cottonwood where the noose swung in the wind.

Behind him in the half-dugout he heard Spradlin say, "You sure he didn't say his name was Fanton?"

"No, he said Stanton. I asked him twice just to make shore."

"Looks a lot like Fanton, don't he?"

"Shore does. That's the main reason I brought him out here. I figgered you'd want a look at him."

"Keep a eye on him and try to find out who he is and what he's doin' here," Spradlin said. "And tell the hands to watch him."

"They been watchin' him like he was a ghost. I almost believe he is, my own self."

The preceding was from the gritty western novel
Dead Man Riding

To keep reading, click or go here:
http://amzn.to/1aknrFD

More hellbound gunslinging westerns by Van Holt:

A Few Dead Men
http://amzn.to/18Xu7ic

Blood in the Hills

http://amzn.to/16jWNvB

Brandon's Law
http://amzn.to/1fijGsy

Buck Haden, Mustanger
Coming Soon!

Curly Bill and Ringo
http://amzn.to/Z6AhSH

Dead Man Riding
http://amzn.to/1aknrFD

Dead Man's Trail
http://amzn.to/ZcPJ47

Death in Black Holsters
http://amzn.to/1aHxGcv

Dynamite Riders
http://amzn.to/ZyhHmg

Hellbound Express
http://amzn.to/11i3NcY

Hunt the Killers Down
http://amzn.to/Z7UHjD

Maben
http://amzn.to/1judfzK

Rebel With A Gun
http://amzn.to/1apARDN

Riding for Revenge
http://amzn.to/13gLILz

Rubeck's Raiders
http://amzn.to/14CDxwU

Shiloh Stark
http://amzn.to/12ZJxcV

Shoot to Kill
http://amzn.to/18zA1qm

Six-Gun Solution
http://amzn.to/10t3H3N

Six-Gun Serenade
http://amzn.to/164cS7t

Six-Gun Showdown
Coming Soon!

Son of a Gunfighter
http://amzn.to/17QAzSp

The Antrim Guns
http://amzn.to/132I7jr

The Bounty Hunters
http://amzn.to/10gJQ6C

The Bushwhackers
http://amzn.to/13ln4JO

The Fortune Hunters
http://amzn.to/11i3VsO

The Gundowners
(formerly So, Long Stranger)
http://amzn.to/16c0I2J

The Gundown Trail
http://amzn.to/1g1jDNs

The Hellbound Man
http://amzn.to/1fTATJy

The Hell Riders
Coming Soon!

The Last of the Fighting Farrells
http://amzn.to/Z6AyVI

The Long Trail
http://amzn.to/137P9c8

The Man Called Bowdry
http://amzn.to/14LjpJa

The Return of Frank Graben
http://amzn.to/1eeiDpk

The Revenge of Sam Graben
Coming Soon!

The Stranger From Hell
http://amzn.to/12qVVqd

The Vultures
http://amzn.to/12bjeGl

Wild Country
http://amzn.to/147xUDq

Wild Desert Rose
http://amzn.to/XH7Y27

Brought to you by Three Knolls Publishing
Independent Publishing in the Digital Age
www.3knollspub.com

About the Author:

Van Holt wrote his first western when he was in high school and sent it to a literary agent, who soon returned it, saying it was too long but he would try to sell it if Holt would cut out 16,000 words. Young Holt couldn't bear to cut out any of his perfect western, so he threw it away and started writing another one.

A draft notice interrupted his plans to become the next Zane Grey or Louis L'Amour. A tour of duty as an MP stationed in South Korea was pretty much the usual MP stuff except for the time he nabbed a North Korean spy and had to talk the dimwitted desk sergeant out of letting the guy go. A briefcase stuffed with drawings of U.S. aircraft and the like only caused the overstuffed lifer behind the counter to rub his fat face, blink his bewildered eyes, and start eating a big candy bar to console himself. Imagine Van Holt's surprise a few days later when he heard that same dumb sergeant telling a group of new admirers how he himself had caught the famous spy one day when he was on his way to the mess hall.

Holt says there hasn't been too much excitement since he got out of the army, unless you count the time he was attacked by two mean young punks and shot one of them in the big toe. Holt believes what we need is punk control, not gun control.

After traveling all over the West and Southwest in an aging Pontiac, Van Holt got tired of traveling the day he rolled into Tucson and he has been there ever since, still dreaming of becoming the next Zane Grey or Louis L'Amour when he grows up. Or maybe the next great mystery writer. He likes to write mysteries when he's not too busy writing westerns or eating Twinkies.

WARNING: Reading a Van Holt western may make you want to get on a horse and hunt some bad guys down in the Old West. Of course, the easiest and most enjoyable way to do it is vicariously – by reading another Van Holt western.

Van Holt writes westerns the way they were meant to be written.

7273126R00096

Printed in Great Britain
by Amazon.co.uk, Ltd.,
Marston Gate.